GRYPHON'S INSTINCT

ELVA BIRCH

A WORLD OF INSTINCT

A Day Care for Shifters is a swoony, sweet-hot series in a World of Instinct set in the small town of Nickel City, where shifters are trying to stay secret…something infinitely complicated by young shifters just learning their magical skills, right along with walking and talking and stealing hearts! These are gentle romances full of humor and feeling, perfect ice-cream-straight-from-the-container escapes.

Start the series with a **3-book collection** that includes *Wolf's Instinct, Dragon's Instinct,* and *Unicorn's Instinct,* plus the short story *First Shift*! Every book stands alone, with a satisfying happy ever after.

Wolf's Instinct: Roderick's toddler daughter and busy plumbing business keep him too wrapped up for romance and while he trusts his wolf, the magic of instinct can be like playing hot-and-cold with a kid who's forgotten where they hid the prize. Addison comes to Nickel City to take a job at a very special day care and finds a family to belong to.

First Comes Love (a mini-series!): Navigating on-line dating is hard enough for a single mom and first shift baker, but Chloe has a whole new set of problems when her little boy suddenly changes into a pushy baby penguin and Clay, a polar bear shifter comes to her rescue. This mini-trilogy includes three short stories: First Shift, First Day, and First Date, all collected with two more bonus stories in First Comes Love, with adorable illustrations by Ellen Million!

Dragon's Instinct: Ian had enough trouble trying to write for a living and keep up with his daughter, Lucy, even before she started shifting into a squirrel. Now that she's turning two and breathing fire? The twos just got a lot more terrible!

Unicorn's Instinct: Tara just wants her mommy to be happy…and a puppy. Vivian doesn't have the heart or time for romance, let alone a puppy, but everything changes when she meets the new pediatric doctor at her clinic and learns his heart-breaking secret.

Gryphon's Instinct: Theo is a single dad chasing two kids—including a teleporting baby gryphon!—and Wendy is just weird enough to fit their family perfectly.

Bearly Better Yeti: *She's looking for a monster…and finds a mate!* Polar bear shifter Oliver got caught on camera at the worst possible time and now Molly Flash, a cryptid-hunting internet celebrity, is snooping around Belle Lake Lodge looking for a yeti. His instinct says she's everything he's ever wanted, but he's got to protect his family's secrets. When Molly goes missing, he risks everything to find her and make her his own. A novella at Belle Lake Lodge.

Stallion's Instinct: He's a playboy, cowboy, and con man… and she's about to get the ride of her life.

Raven's Instinct: Ravens like shiny things…

You can also get signed and sketched paperbacks!

CHAPTER 1

*L*eaving the emergency room at midnight on Halloween was not Theo's idea of a good time.

He wasn't sure how it could get any worse until he drove up in front of his house and found a familiar car parked in the slushy snow by the curb.

"Is that Mom's car?" Theo's twelve-year-old son, Darius, asked in astonishment.

Theo wasn't sure how Juliette could have gotten to Nickel City, Montana from Las Vegas, Nevada so quickly, even if the school had somehow called her. His texts to her from the hospital waiting room had gone unread.

Theo pulled up the drive. By the time he'd walked around the truck, Darius had struggled, one-handed, out of his seat and his feet were on the snowy ground, his braced wrist cradled in the other.

Juliette had gotten out as well, and gone to the back seat for a covered car seat she slung easily over her arm as they all met in the middle of the driveway.

"Mom?" Darius said, hanging back. It had been six

months since they'd seen each other, and he obviously couldn't decide if he should be mad or happy.

Seeing them at the same time made Theo realize all at once how tall Darius had gotten in the year they'd been in Nickel City. He looked a lot like his mother, even if Darius had gotten Theo's dark hair and not Juliette's dark blonde locks.

"What's wrong with your wrist, honey?" Juliette asked.

Darius shrugged and scuffed a foot in the snow.

"Darius just took a nosedive off the bleachers at school," Theo said, choosing not to share his suspicion that he'd been pushed in front of Darius. "It's just sprained. But I'm guessing that's not why you're here." He tried not to stare at the car seat. If she was here, with Jackson…

"Jackson has started shifting," Juliette said without preamble. "I'm sorry to do this to you, Theo, but you're going to have to take him."

"He's—"

"A gryphon," Juliette said. "Like his dad." It was dark and the only light was from a dim streetlight and a small porch fixture; Theo couldn't make out her expression.

But he could feel the muted little tingle of magic from the quiet, covered car seat as Juliette thrust it at him.

"I've brought his things," she said, turning back to the car.

Jackson. Theo clutched the car seat against himself.

He and Juliette had been separated for several years in Las Vegas, but she stayed in touch with Darius and showed up for important events and milestones…and sometimes, catching up on the couch after their son had gone to bed, it was too easy to slip into old habits.

When Jackson was the natural result of one of those old habits, they'd discussed getting back together, but between Juliette's secrecy and the draw of Theo's instinct, he'd chosen instead to move to Nickel City with Darius to start over on his own. Darius had never started shifting, and if Theo had known that the baby—Jackson!—would, he might have fought harder for custody. But Juliette had wanted Jackson, Darius had been deeply opinionated about staying with Theo, and Theo wasn't sure he could handle two children on his own.

Now, whether he was ready for it or not, it looked like he was going to have to.

Theo took the car seat into the house and set it on the floor by the couch, crouching beside it. After a moment, he unzipped the fleece cover.

The baby had a short shock of dark hair, and he was sleeping in that boneless way that babies had, head kinked over to one side in an impossibly uncomfortable-looking position. A fist was clutching a plastic snail clipped to the car seat, and it was tiny, with tiny little nails. Eyelashes spread over fat cheeks and his little mouth was just parted. His eyebrows were so faint and so expressive, even in sleep.

He was so helpless and so *perfect*.

Theo's gryphon swelled with pride. *Our little gryphon.*

What did this mean? How could one glance fill up Theo's heart so completely? Would it trouble his relationship with Darius? Complicate his relationship with Juliette? What was he going to do about *work*?

He looked up to find that Darius had followed him quietly in and was staring down at Jackson with the same wonder and confusion on his face.

The door had been left ajar behind him and Juliette pushed it open with her arms full of boxes and bags, letting a cold draft in with her. Theo got to his feet and went to help her find a place to put them, as quietly as possible so that Jackson could sleep.

It took several trips from Juliette's car to transfer all of

Jackson's things. There were so many parts of having a baby that Theo had all but forgotten about: the folding playpen-crib, the bouncy chair, the case of diapers, the sippy cups and plastic spoons, toys, blankets, and bags of clothing.

"He's on solid food," Juliette said, "and pulling himself up. He's probably close to walking. He's had his six month shots and met all his eight month milestones. He's got some sounds that are like words but not quite. He loves car rides and they put him to sleep, and the purple dinosaur stuffy is his favorite. He likes peas and most vegetables, soft chicken, and milk. He won't eat pasta, which is a little weird, but he likes bread."

"Juliette…" Theo stopped her in the driveway when the car was empty. Darius had remained inside, not able to help carry anything with his hurt wrist.

He could tell that Juliette wasn't happy about having to do this. Whatever other problems they'd had, she loved her kids and was a wonderful mom. She wouldn't be giving up Jackson lightly. But she only glanced at the front door and wistfully said, "How's Darius doing?"

"Except for dramatically spraining his wrist in the middle of a Halloween party tonight, he's been really good. Great grades, has friends, gets embarrassed around girls. What's going on here?" Theo was sure he was only getting half a story. Juliette had always been reticent to share her life with him, but she seemed particularly mysterious now.

"I'm not a shifter," Juliette reminded him. "I can't keep him a secret like you can."

"Don't lie to me, Juliette," Theo said fiercely. "Not with our kids at stake. What's really going on?"

Juliette's face in the unflattering light of the streetlamp was drawn and after a moment of meeting his eyes defiantly, she gave a sigh of surrender. "There are...some things going on with my job and Jackson will be *safer* with you."

"I'm going to need some more details than that," Theo said. He could feel his gryphon puffing up in concern. There was an undeniable undercurrent of worry, but he'd just been through a big scare with Darius and he wasn't sure what was lingering adrenaline and what was instinct.

Juliette's mouth worked without words for a moment and then went into a tight line. "I'm not allowed to tell you."

Frustration swamped his unease.

"This is my family, Juliette. I'm not going to take some line of bullsh—"

"Do you think I wouldn't tell you if I could?" Juliette snapped back. "They're my kids, too, Theo, and I wouldn't do anything to put them in danger. They'll be safe here, with you, and Jackson wouldn't be in Vegas with me, and if that's not enough for you, well, there's nothing I can do about that."

Theo gritted his teeth and tried to make sense of everything. Between swirling emotions and what felt like a complete upset of his life, it was hard to pick instinct out from outrage and worry. It was also hard to decide what was his own desire. He worried he was missing out on Jackson's life, frequently fretting that he'd made a mistake in moving away and cutting ties. Juliette sent him perfunctory photographs and updates, and every one of them came with a niggling doubt that he'd ultimately made the wrong choice in giving Jackson up to her.

Juliette's voice was gentle, but firm. "I know you're a great dad. You always have been. Jackson needs *you*. You weren't expecting this, and I'm sorry to dump it all on you at once with no warning, but…I'm sure you can agree this is what's best for him."

Theo had no argument for that. "You could have texted me."

"It was too important to say by text," Juliette said. "I'll give you a new number to use if you need to contact me. I'll be in touch about child support."

"How much danger is Jackson in?" Theo fished his phone out of his pocket and updated her number. "How much danger are *you* in?"

"I'm fine," Juliette assured him. "And Jackson will be fine *here*."

"You aren't planning to drive back to Vegas tonight, are you?"

"I need to get back to work before I'm missed," Juliette said evenly. "We both napped waiting for you to get home, and I'll snatch a few hours of sleep in the car on the way back if I need to. Don't worry about me."

Theo wrestled with his need for more information. He knew from experience that Juliette would give him exactly as much as she thought he needed to know…and not a shred more. They could argue longer, or… "You want a cup of coffee first?" he asked wearily.

Juliette gave him a slow, tired smile. "I'd like that. It'll give me a chance to catch up with Darius and find out why he thought spraining his wrist was a good idea."

Maybe Juliette could get more out of him than Theo had. They crept quietly into the house, and found that Jackson had woken up while they were getting the last of his things.

Darius was holding the baby in his good arm, making goofy faces and bouncing him slightly against him. Jackson was bubbling with laughter, grabbing at Darius's hospital band.

"Who's a baby?" Darius said, deftly catching Jackson's hand and letting him wrap tiny fingers around the thumb sticking from his brace. "Ouch! Careful! You're the baby!" He tipped his head forward and touched Jackson's forehead gently with his own. "Baby brother!"

They were a domestic picture of affection and all of Theo's worries that Jackson would be unwelcome in their little family vanished in the face of Darius's obvious tenderness.

Theo glanced over to see Juliette's face relax in the same relief that he was feeling.

Darius turned just far enough to see that they had come inside and went stiff and embarrassed, but he didn't offer to let go of the baby. "Hey," he said with a shrug. "Jackson woke up. No big deal."

Theo didn't need instinct to tell him that this was a very big deal indeed.

CHAPTER 2

*W*endy was pretty sure she was in hell, and that hell was the sweltering, hormone-heavy gym of Nickel City Middle School for Career Day.

There were still Halloween decorations left up from the weekend before; a ghost fluttered above the basketball hoop, and orange and black streamers were taped at ladder-height along the ceiling. The room didn't have great acoustics, and it was loud with shouts and laughter and people trying to have normal conversations over all the noise.

Tables and informational displays from local Nickel City businesses lined the perimeter of the gym, and reluctant kids on the cusp or in the throes of puberty were being forced to visit each one. An enterprising teacher had decided to require the kids to get stamps at each station for asking a question of every bored business representative.

The people-watching was more engrossing than Wendy had expected it to be, and she amused herself by observing the social swirls of the youngsters. There were the nerds, making their methodical way along the tables to get their validations. The jocks bounced around, using the excuse of being in the gym to be loud and ricochet off of each other. Popular girls giggled their way to tables spelling out futures that were too distant to be relevant and self-consciously checked their hair and skirts and shoes. The range of ages and maturities was fantastic, with kids who looked a step out of kindergarten rubbing elbows with teens who might be able to buy cigarettes if the clerk wasn't checking identification carefully.

And, ah! There were the shifters!

Wendy wasn't a shifter herself and didn't have magical instinct to tell her for sure who was, but she knew enough about the secret community to make an educated guess. This cluster of kids ranged in age, gender, and race. They looked athletic, but weren't in with the jocks. They had a sense of reserve that was rare in kids of this age, and shifters often grouped together in class-defying social circles. Wendy entertained herself by speculating about what their shift forms were while they were getting treats and stamps at the next table. The tallest one seemed like their ringleader, and Wendy guessed he was a bear or a lion. There was one boy on their fringes with a brace on his wrist, and Wendy wondered why he looked slightly out of place. Maybe it was just that shifters so rarely got injured or sick.

Kids came to her table last and most reluctantly, and Wendy knew why.

It wasn't just that she was representing the DMV, the dullest and least respectable of the professions on display. It was Wendy herself.

Nickel City was a small town, and Wendy was loud and outspoken. She was constantly at war with her homeowners association, and she didn't take anything lying down. This didn't exactly endear her to the public, and she wasn't oblivious to the whispers and sidelong glances as the students filled each other in on tales of her exploits and descriptions of her oddities. '*Weirdo*,' would be the least of their titles for her...and these kids were at an age where *weirdo* was a top-level insult as they strove for conformity and confidence.

She was perfectly happy to live up to every inch of her reputation, and she smiled as the rag-tag group of probably-shifters approached her table.

The maybe-bear boy pushed his paper across the table without comment and poked disinterestedly at the safe driving stickers.

"What's your question?" Wendy asked pleasantly, toying with her stamp.

"None of the other tables are actually making us ask questions," the prepubescent kid across from her protested.

"Yeah," the tomboy beside him added. "They just give us pens and keychains and stamp our papers."

"The point of a career fair is to make you realize that there's no such thing as a free ride," Wendy said. "You ask me a decent question, and I'll stamp your paper."

"The other tables have chocolate, too," one kid whined.

"I'm not bribing you to work at the DMV," Wendy countered. "I'm appealing to your sense of self-preservation." Did that sound too much like a threat? A shrimpy little boy looked pale and afraid. Maybe he was a rodent of some kind. "Ask me a valid question and I'll stamp your participation paper."

The probably-bear groaned and eyed the sign behind Wendy. "What benefits do you get working at the DMV?" he intoned.

"Bravo," Wendy said. She glanced at the name on his form: Brandon T. "The state of Montana has a generous retirement program, comprehensive health insurance, full dental and vision, and three weeks of paid leave from your first year, Brandon. Next?"

"Suck-up," someone muttered.

"What he said," one of his friends said, waving his form. "That's my question, too." His name was Keaton M. What was with the fancy names that kids got these days? She rarely saw Freds and Steves and Toms in the younger generations.

"I'm not stamping your paper for hanging on your friend's coattails," Wendy said, giving Brandon's paper a stamp with a cartoon car. "Think of your own question."

Brandon smirked and edged back triumphantly while the others all groaned.

"Uh, how much does it pay?" Keaton asked.

Wendy shuffled the pay scale to the top of her pile of visual aids. "It's a sliding scale salary based on longevity and rank. As an employee of the state, you can apply your time in service to any of their many career opportunities." She didn't blame Keaton for staring blankly at the crowded printout and stamped his form without making him do the math to figure out the hourly wage.

The next kid, Sophia, asked about working hours, and Wendy gave the one after, Noah Q., credit for asking more specifically about lunch breaks. "I ought to give you half a stamp for that," she said, but she gave it a solid stamp and they both moved back away from the table in relief.

The remaining shifter pre-teens looked desperate as they ran out of decent questions. "Can you get out of parking tickets?"

"Nope," Wendy said, but she stamped Taylor T.'s form, because it was a valid question. "You still have to be a law-abiding citizen."

"Can you speed?" the next one asked hopefully.

"That question is too derivative," Wendy said scornfully. "No credit."

The quiet one with a wrist brace asked, "Is it any *fun* at all?"

Wendy had to pause, no answer ready for that particular question. He met her gaze without flinching or looking away, which most kids wouldn't do. He had brownish golden eyes, an unusual eye color that was another giveaway that he was a shifter. The only girl that Wendy had ever met with actual violet eyes had been a shifter, and most of Wendy's family had bright golden-green eyes.

"It's a necessary service for fair pay." Wendy recognized her reply for the dodge that it was when she heard the words and tried again. "It's fun interacting with interesting people and helping them navigate the system. I like my boss and I enjoy keeping people out of trouble. You can make anything exciting if you try to."

"Coo-coo," someone muttered from behind the kid, and he ducked his head and looked abashed.

Wendy stamped wrist-brace's form. His name was Darius R. Another one of those ritzy names. "That was a good question."

She held onto his form just long enough that he had to meet her eyes again, and he scowled at her impressively. Maybe he was a wolverine. Something grumpy, for sure.

"Oh my God, she is such a weirdo," Wendy heard one of the kids stage-whisper as the last of them left in a cliquish cluster. "I heard she gave out raisins and toothpaste at Halloween."

"And yelled at kids about brushing their teeth!"

"I heard she bites the heads off of bats."

"That's Ozzy Osbourne," another scoffed.

"What a freak."

Wendy wasn't sure if that was in reference to Ozzy Osbourne or herself, but she felt a certain amount of both chagrin and gratification at the label. She'd rather be herself than a hundred other people.

Most of the time.

CHAPTER 3

"It's time to go!" Theo hollered.

Leaving the house had become an act of acrobatics and desperation in the last week, between Darius and his sprained wrist, and the sudden addition of an eight-month-old baby who might turn into a gryphon at any unexpected moment.

Jackson was squalling now, and protesting…well, Theo wasn't sure what he was protesting. It could be a diaper or a hunger pang or a bad taste in his mouth or just a general complaint about the state of the world. Maybe he was teething. Or beaking. Or whatever a gryphon did. Theo didn't have time to investigate it.

"Darius, we need to *leave*! School starts in ten minutes!"

"Geez, Dad, sorry I'm so *slow*."

Theo was not sure how Darius managed to pack that much sarcasm into six words, but it was masterfully done as the twelve-year-old boy waved his braced hand in reminder.

"Start earlier," Theo suggested. "I got you up with plenty of time."

There was nothing he could do about Darius moping and his very selective pretense that his wrist brace made him incapable of basic tasks, and Theo had changed Jackson's diaper three times in the last hour and tried him on four refused foods and all of his toys.

"It's not that big of a deal to be late," Darius said.

"It's that big of a deal when I have to drag Jackson into your school to sign you in late," Theo reminded him. "You know he's a shift-risk."

"So I'll skip school," Darius said flippantly.

"You're not *skipping school!*" Theo checked Jackson's bag. He was going to have to buy more diapers soon. How could something so tiny make so many terrible messes? He'd forgotten a lot about babies since Darius was one. "Let's go."

"I don't have my lunch made yet."

It took every shred of Theo's self-control not to swear. "You were supposed to make it after breakfast while I was in the shower."

Darius waved his wrist brace again.

"That gets you out of doing dishes, but I think you can put a slab of cheese on a slice of bread with one hand. There's no time now. You'll have to buy a hot lunch."

Darius groaned. "No, Dad! It's gross and no one cool eats hot lunch. I'm in *middle school.*"

"Then I guess you'll be cool and starve. Go get your books."

Darius made a show of struggling to get his backpack over his shoulder, though Theo had seen him do it one-handed a hundred times before he'd injured himself. With Jackson's diaper bag hung on one arm and the car seat over the other, Theo hustled them all out the front door and locked the door.

Darius took as long to buckle himself in as it took Theo

to get Jackson, still wailing, into the car seat dock and shut the back door of the truck before climbing into his own seat.

"How much do you need for lunch?" Theo asked, as he tried not to speed through the quiet neighborhood. The last thing he needed was a ticket.

"I don't want hot lunch," Darius complained.

"You have to eat lunch!" Theo argued. Why was this even a discussion? Had he been half this difficult as a child?

"I'll get something from the vending machine," Darius suggested.

"A bag of chips and a coke are not lunch!"

"They have, like, Hot Pockets and things!"

Jackson, who had quieted as they drove, gave a burp and then began crying again, beating his fists on the tray of his car seat. "Abababababababa!"

Theo turned into the school parking lot too sharply, and the truck went up on the curb. He hoped no one noticed as he pulled up to drop Darius off, coming to a stop behind a tiny Subaru with a half dozen kids piling out. Theo dug into his wallet and found a ten-dollar bill. "Buy the healthiest thing they have," he ordered.

"Sure, Dad!" Darius said cheerfully. He had no trouble unbuckling or getting out of the truck with his backpack, having forgotten how helpless he was supposed to be. Theo ground his teeth in frustration and put the truck in gear, then smashed on the brakes and put the truck in neutral as he noticed a figure getting out of the car behind him, waving for him to stop.

The woman ran forward, her hands like celebration flags at the ends of her arms, and Theo put the window down at her approach. "Oh, sorry!" she said eagerly. "It's just, I noticed your tags were expired and wanted to warn you!"

Theo looked towards the rear of his truck as if he could possibly see his tags from his seat and gave a groan. "I appreciate the warning, ma'am," he said as politely as possible.

The mother flashed him an inviting smile. "Call me Regina! I wouldn't want you to get a ticket!" she said cheerfully. "The cops in this town are something, don't you think?"

"Yes, ma'am," Theo said. "I'm sure they wouldn't hesitate to pull me over."

Regina laughed as if he'd said something very funny and leaned into the truck a little further. "Maybe we could get coffee sometime and compare speed traps," she suggested. "Let me give you my number…"

To his surprise, there was a tingle of apprehension, and his gryphon suddenly stirred inside of him. *We have somewhere else to be. Now!*

Instinct wasn't often that specific. It was usually a warning or a niggling little feeling that something was wrong. Sometimes, it was a sinking feeling that had no particular source, or a sudden uneasiness. Every once in a while, it was a bolt of intuition to trust someone or to get out of the way.

This was weirdly different, and Theo glanced back to where Jackson was quietly whimpering. Was the baby going to shift? Were they in danger of exposing their secret? The rear windows of the truck were tinted, but he wasn't sure the car seat buckles would hold a truly determined baby gryphon.

Jackson was at a highly unpredictable age, and Theo hadn't even seen him as a gryphon yet. His own gryphon's tingle of instinct told him that the boy was a shifter, but the sense was quiet now, like a simmering pot, not a lid-bouncing boil.

Regina was staring at him in concern. "Is something wrong? Oh, how old is your baby?" She craned to see behind him and Theo let instinct take the literal wheel.

"I'm sorry, ma'am, Regina, I'm running late. We're blocking the way. Time to go!" Theo babbled through a choice of excuses and put the truck in gear. The Subaru in front of him was long gone.

Regina stepped back in alarm as he peeled out of the parking lot before he remembered that speeding and getting pulled over with expired tags was probably a very bad idea.

Jackson chortled from the back seat.

But Theo had ninety-nine problems, starting with a sullen almost-teenager with a sprained wrist, a fussy baby who might turn into a fuzzy gryphon at any moment, and expired tags on his truck. His instinct was guiding him to the DMV.

CHAPTER 4

endy didn't work at the DMV because she loved being yelled at, which was too bad. She suspected she'd have a lot more job satisfaction if she did. She thought wryly about the wrist-braced boy's question at the Career Fair from the week before. She supposed that there was *some* amount of fun in dealing with Nickel City's most unhinged, such as Mr. Charles Vissey Smith, who insisted on being called by his entire name every time, as if he'd paid for each extra letter on his license.

"I'm sorry ,Mr. Charles Vissey Smith, I can't issue you a new driver's license until you pass the vision test. This is not me being a stickler for rules. Go get your glasses updated and I'll stamp your papers and take your photo."

"It's a conspiracy, that's what it is!" Mr. Charles Vissey Smith protested. "They don't want God-fearing men like me on the roads. It's all you women with your pink hats who want to oppress us and put us in kitchens while you drive the government into the ground."

Wendy, who had knit about a dozen of those pink hats when they were the rage, would have happily put one on at that moment if it would oppress Mr. Charles Vissey Smith in the slightest.

"I promise you, it's just about your vision test," Wendy said, mustering all of her patience. "Otherwise, you'd walk out of here with a license just like everyone else who came in, regardless of your gender or *hat color*."

"It wasn't like this when we had a real president in office!" Mr. Charles Vissey Smith growled. "Decent, law-abiding citizens. They're trying to subject us to medical experimentation and control. They let aliens into this country and the whole place went to hell. Did you know that there are people here who change into *animals*?"

Wendy might have baited him in ranting further, just for fun. *Was it a women's conspiracy? The federal government's fault? Immigration?* But suggesting that there were shapeshifters in Nickel City got a little too close to the truth. She kept her voice dry and full of disbelief. "Shapeshifters, you say? That's very interesting. Next?"

Nickel City's sole DMV office was not usually so busy that there were long lines. Most of the department's services were available online now and the days of crowds out the door were over. Mostly, Wendy had the office completely to herself and got only the very desperate and last-minute jobs—licenses that were already expired, tags that would get them pulled over. And people like Mr. Charles Vissey Smith, who believed the Internet would steal his soul. Or maybe it was immigrants stealing his soul. Did he mean aliens like the Space Invaders video game? Wendy honestly didn't know.

Even if Wendy didn't miss the hordes of humanity, she was glad to see that another customer had come in, a car seat hanging on his forearm, because it gave her an excuse to move Mr. Charles Vissey Smith along.

He went grumbling off, probably to drive with his

expired license, and Wendy gestured at the dad, who was hanging politely back past the "Wait Here For the Next Available Agent" sign.

The first thing Wendy noticed about him were his movie star good looks.

He had a scruffy bit of half-grown beard that did nothing to hide the fact that he had a strong, symmetrical jaw and a sultry mouth. Men weren't supposed to have mouths that sexy. They also weren't supposed to have eyes that dreamy and golden. How was it fair that he had eyelashes so long and dark without mascara? Was he actually *wearing* mascara, or was he just that pretty?

The second thing Wendy noticed about him was that he was trying to hide the car seat, or whatever was in it. The fleece cover kicked out in protest, and the squawk from within was half chirp and half growl.

Was he one of those weirdos who had a small bite-y dog they were trying to pass off as a service animal? In a car seat? Maybe it was a parrot.

Wendy shrugged. It took all kinds, and after Mr. Charles Vissey Smith, she was happy to ignore smuggled animals. She wasn't with the department of Fish, Wildlife, and Parks. She just had to rubber stamp licenses and keep people off the roads who couldn't see.

"How can I help you?" she asked cheerfully.

"Tags! Expired!" The movie star was staring at Wendy in frank alarm and surprise, his brow furrowed in confusion.

"Got your registration and license?" Wendy prodded him, when he seemed to get no further in the process than those two words.

"Right! Yes! Here!"

He got the car seat up on the counter and held it in place as he thrust his entire wallet across to her, along with a folded paper that proved to be his truck registration.

Wendy, after a moment of hesitation regarding his privacy, opened the wallet and slid out his driver's license. A credit card came with it, and a folded receipt.

His name was Theodore Royal, and his driver's license was from Nevada. Even his name sounded like a movie star, and his picture had a smoldering half-smile. "This expires in two weeks," she said, reminding herself to stop drooling over his photograph.

He looked absolutely panicked, his arms flung over the car seat like he was trying to hold something in.

Then he stared at her suspiciously, and after a moment of hard regard, his features melted in relief. "You're a shifter!" He immediately glanced around, probably looking for surveillance.

Wendy felt a pang of regret overwhelm her libido. "Actually not," she said. "I'm just an anomaly. But I know about shifters and I'll keep your secret. The security cameras are just for show. My boss takes a lot of breaks she doesn't really want on tape. Who's in the car seat? Or should I say what?"

Theodore Royal uncovered the struggling baby and a stronger woman than Wendy would have melted. "Oh, what a cutie!"

No parent could resist praise for their child, and Wendy wasn't exaggerating in the least. She thought it was a bird shifter baby at first, with a snapping beak and downy wings, but then it wriggled half out of the straps that had been made to restrain an ordinary baby, and Wendy saw it had a tufted lion's tail and hind legs with toe beans and tiny needle-sharp claws. A romper lay in pieces around him, as well as a torn diaper.

"A gryphon!" she cooed. "Who's the darlingest thing ever?"

Theodore Royal, perhaps, Wendy answered herself internally. He was smiling in foolish relief now, and it made him more handsome than worry did.

Wendy wasn't a shifter, and she didn't have instinct, but she knew someone in trouble when she saw it, and this guy had a whole pile of trouble on his hands. A whole cute pile of trouble in the form of a baby gryphon. "Have you heard about Tiny Paws?" she said impulsively. "It's a day care for shifters."

CHAPTER 5

Theo wasn't sure what to make of Wendy.

He never would have guessed she was his type, with her wild, frizzy, silver-streaked strawberry-blonde hair, but she had an earthy kind of attractiveness and a direct gaze that Theo found enchanting. She wore a black fluttering blouse and a chunky gemstone necklace, but no makeup. She looked like a Bohemian goth who'd left the house in a hurry, like no box in the world could hold her.

She was smiling, and there was something about her that made him feel like he was exactly where he ought to be, like he didn't have to be anything he wasn't.

Was it instinct? If it was, he couldn't figure out what it was trying to tell him. She had that slight tingle of a fellow shifter, but then she'd said—a little sadly?—that she wasn't one.

His gryphon was interested in her, in the focused way of a predator, but he could make no more sense of that fascination than Theo could. *Complicated*, was all he could offer.

They both agreed that she felt *safe*, and she'd offered them a solution to Jackson's care that he had despaired of finding.

"A day care for shifters?"

"Have you been in town long?" Wendy asked. "Haven't you noticed that there are a lot of shifters around?"

"I moved here at the end of last year," Theo said. "Wow, is it November already? I've…been a little busy, and Jackson's mother had custody of him until last week."

It was a gross oversimplification, and Theo was astonished to find himself desperate to explain. "Not that I didn't want custody. I mean, I never asked for it, but we already had a son and he's a handful. He's twelve, so you know that age. Maybe you know. And Juliette wanted the baby, and I didn't see how I could take them both. But then, *this*. He's shifting now, and I honestly didn't think he would because Darius never did, but Juliette didn't know what to do with a *gryphon*. And…oh my god, I'm so sorry, I just need to get my truck tags and I didn't mean to overshare."

The events of the last week seemed to crash down on him all at once, and Theo was rocked by the strength of everything he'd been avoiding thinking about for a long, desperate, sleepless week.

"Hey, hey…"

To Theo's surprise, Wendy reached across the counter and took his free hand in hers. The shifter-tingle intensified with her touch. "It's okay," she said gently. "Kids are a lot, and it sounds like you've had a bunch of surprises lately. Pretend I'm your bartender and tell me about it while you fill out these forms. I can hold Jackson if you need both hands."

"Do you have kids?" Theo asked, juggling a wriggling Jackson in one arm as he tried to figure out how to best pass him over the counter. He realized he was clasping Wendy's hand back, comforted by her kind touch.

"Nope," Wendy said merrily, escaping from his hand before he could make it weird to reach for Jackson. "But I know which end goes up and I'm okay at not dropping them. Can he fly?"

"I haven't tested that yet," Theo admitted, passing the fluffy gryphon chick to her. "This is the first time he's shifted with me."

"Everything's new and wonderful!" Wendy cooed.

Theo wasn't sure if she was talking to him, or to Jack, who chirped back at her and stared curiously in that *figuring-you-out* way that babies often had with strangers. Then Jackson gave a bird belch and shifted back into a naked human baby. A few downy feathers escaped the transformation.

Wendy deftly caught him before he could slip through her grasp without feathers and wings, and gathered him fearlessly up against her. "If you pee on me, I'm citing you for harassing a state employee," she warned him.

Jackson chortled, grabbed for her hair, and yanked it hard.

"Sorry," Theo said, not sure if he should try to take Jackson back.

"I have plenty of hair," Wendy said. "No worries." She teased Jackson's fingers away from her curls and bounced him at her hip. "Who's a grabby little boy?" She glanced over at Theo, who realized he was staring rudely again. "Your name goes on the top line. It's Theodore Royal, in case you'd forgotten." She said it with a snobby British accent.

Theo chuckled and took one of the DMV pens to scrawl his information onto the form as quickly as possible. "Theo," he told her. "Just Theo."

"So, tell me your troubles, Theo," Wendy said, giving Jackson a pen. "Not for your mouth, kiddo," she said, quickly realizing the problem with that as a toy. She swapped it out for a teething ring from Jackson's car seat. Jackson eagerly alternated gumming it and hitting Wendy with it.

Theo laughed humorlessly. "Where do I start? Darius, that's my older son, sprained his wrist at a Halloween carnival and scared the spit out of me, and that same night I had a surprise visit from my ex with the news that our eight-month-old baby had turned into a gryphon and is now suddenly *my* problem. She's got…a job that keeps her really busy…and it wasn't going to *stay* a secret for very long."

"I imagine that a baby gryphon is a lot to handle," Wendy said wryly. "Let's not hit the nice lady who's trying to keep your dad from getting a ticket, Jackson!"

"Believe me, it is," Theo said briefly. He glanced up to find Wendy looking sympathetically at him and swiftly added, "It's not like I'm pining over her or anything. We're not together. It's not like that. I'm *single*." He wasn't sure why it was so imperative that Wendy know that.

She only looked amused. And slightly battered by Jackson, who would only stop hitting her for a few moments at a time.

"Do you want the form for a driver's license, too?" Wendy offered. "You are technically required to have a Montana state license within 60 days of living here, you know, and if your out-of-state driver's license expires before you get one, you have to take the driving test again."

"I'd better," Theo agreed.

For a woman who didn't have kids, she was very good at keeping Jackson's grabbing fingers from the forms and at entertaining him as she passed another several sheets across the counter to Theo. He dutifully filled them out.

"Do you have proof of residency with you?" Wendy asked, standing Jackson up on the counter to bounce in place with her help. "You need clothes, naked baby! It's too cold outside to be naked!"

"I've got a change of clothes in the diaper bag." Theo looked around for it and realized he'd left it in the truck. "I just have to…ah…could you watch him for a moment?"

Jackson had gotten another handful of Wendy's hair.

"Ow! No problem!" she said, wincing and smiling. "I didn't really need all that hair!"

When he got back with Jackson's bag, she had come around from behind the desk and was twirling around the lobby with Jackson in her arms. He was happily giggling and flailing his arms and legs. He shrieked and grabbed at her whenever she changed directions.

Theo had to stop at the door to the DMV and stare at them.

Wendy's flowing clothing and wild hair seemed absolutely perfect for the moment, like she'd dressed for a dance. Her head bent lovingly over Jackson's mop of dark hair, and she was holding him with a perfect mix of strength and gentleness. Her laughter mixed with his like music, and something in Theo's chest that he hadn't known was there eased into contentment.

The exhaustion and stress and uncertainty that had plagued him since Darius threw himself off the bleachers and Juliette arrived with Jackson seemed unimportant in the moment. They would get through this, he thought.

Wendy was like…hope.

His gryphon gave a sigh of contentment, and instinct seemed to hum happily.

She caught sight of him and stopped spinning, looking

sheepish. "Oh, I thought it would take you longer to get that. Ahem. Yes, here I am, a very serious state employee. Can I stamp something for you?"

Theo had to laugh, because he could already tell that nothing about Wendy could ever be *serious*. "I had a phone bill in the truck, too. Will that count as proof of residency?"

"I'll trade you," Wendy said, offering him Jackson. "The best thing about other people's babies is that you can give them back."

This tradeoff was considerably more fraught than the first one had been, because they were standing without the protection of a counter between them. Theo was uncomfortably aware of her warmth and proximity as she handed him Jack, peeling his little fingers from the ruffles of her blouse. "Sorry!" she said, laughing, as Jack pulled hard enough to show Theo a glimpse of tantalizing cleavage.

Theo had seen plenty of breasts in his days in Las Vegas; he wasn't sure why this modest peek at Wendy's curves had such an effect on him. Maybe because she *wasn't* trying to show them to him?

He only knew that everything about her absolutely enraptured him, and that instinct was telling him that he'd come home at last.

CHAPTER 6

endy tried not to stare too much at Theo as he dressed Jackson and made goofy faces at him. He might have only just gotten custody of his baby, but he clearly knew what he was doing with one.

Wendy had heard the phrase *made my ovaries explode* and always thought that it was a little gross and unlikely, but that seemed to be exactly what was happening to her now. It wasn't that she suddenly wanted kids of her own, but watching Theo with Jackson made her feel unreasonably weak and squishy inside.

Maybe it was just Theo making things somewhat lower than her ovaries light on fire. He was utterly breathtaking, and Wendy had to force herself back to her job several times instead of watching him and wishing he was wearing a little less. He seemed very strong, but the puffy coat he was wearing hid his figure. He certainly had nice legs beneath it, and nice hands, and nice eyes…

"Unfortunately, I can't use your phone bill because you only have a PO Box listed for your billing address. Do you have an electric or landline bill with a house address on it?"

"Not in the truck, sorry."

"Make sure you come back with one before the twenty-eighth or I'll have to require a driving test, and I tell you, the person who runs those is a real bear."

Theo looked at her suspiciously. "A real bear?"

"It's me, I'm the bear. Not a real bear." Wendy feared for a moment that she'd made too terrible a joke and was glad when he laughed.

She was even more glad when he blurted, "Do you want to go out sometime? For dinner?"

"I'd like that!" Wendy said, too eagerly. *Down, girl, don't scare him off.* "I'm free tomorrow night." She was free tonight, too, but it seemed a little desperate of her to say that.

"How about The Miner's Grill?" Theo suggested.

The Miner's Grill was a modest place with a broad menu, a liquor license, and comfortable booths. It wasn't that fancy, but it wasn't a dive bar, either. Wendy approved of the choice. "At six?"

"I'll make a reservation."

Wendy wasn't sure The Miner's Grill really required a reservation, but honestly, she wasn't sure how dating even worked anymore. "I'll meet you there," she said. *Always play a first date cautiously and have an escape plan.* "We can go dutch. Do people still say that? Is it painfully obvious that I haven't dated in a while?"

Theo chuckled indulgently. "Me neither. I'll see you there. At six!"

"That sounds great." Wendy was not awesome at sounding nonchalant, but she did her best. She also applauded her inner editor for not pointing out that

Jackson was proof that he'd clearly gotten laid a lot more recently than she had and making a competition out of it.

When Jackson was dressed, Wendy wished she had more paperwork to hand over the counter at his dad. Maybe some forms to stamp. There was a lot there she'd like to stamp. There was a jangle at the door and Theo looked nervously over his shoulder and then gathered Jackson into his arms. "Thanks for your help," he said, trying to pull Jackson's hood up over his face as if that would shield the view if he turned into a gryphon.

Jackson wanted nothing to do with that and gave a squawk of protest.

Theo bundled him up and hurried to the door, then had to rush back to the counter when Wendy called him back to get his wallet.

The next customer, an elderly woman in an old wool coat, was considerably less exciting—and far less sexy. Wendy was glad when she finished her business and shuffled out so that Wendy could impulsively call her cousin Addison.

"I have a date," she blurted. "Help, what do I do?"

Addison gave a squeal. "What? Who is it? When?"

Wendy immediately regretted calling. "Tomorrow night. Dammit, I forgot to give him my phone number."

In the world's worst or best timing, the DMV phone rang. "Sorry to get your hopes up, I have to answer this, see you and Dana at lunch on Saturday! Bye!"

She studiously avoided her cellphone the rest of the day and refused to open her texts to see how many eggplant emoticons Addison had sent her.

CHAPTER 7

It wasn't that Theo had forgotten about Jackson when he made the date with Wendy. He'd just forgotten all the scheduling things that came with having a baby. Darius had been old enough to stay home for a few hours by himself for several years now, and it surprised Theo how willingly he had stepped up to help care for Jackson. Darius had already stayed home with the baby several times by himself so Theo could go to work in the evening. But a work shift so that they could pay bills was a lot different than a date.

"Darius, my dude," Theo started expansively.

Darius shot him a deeply suspicious look. "What do you want, Dad?"

"I have a date tomorrow night. Will you please watch Jackson for a few hours?" Theo just barely avoided begging.

Darius looked intrigued. "I don't have anything going on. Who is she?"

"Her name is Wendy," Theo said, remembering how

she'd danced around with Jackson, and her friendly grin across the counter, full of life and humor.

"Wendy," Darius said suspiciously. "Just Wendy? How'd you meet?"

"Wendy Carmichael," Theo said, remembering her name plate. "She works at the DMV. Jackson shifted right when we got there and she absolutely saved our bacon."

Darius was looking at him in horror.

"It's okay. Instinct said she was safe, and I could feel that she was a shifter, even though—"

"Wendy from the DMV?" Darius interrupted Theo, looking like he'd found something bad-tasting in his mouth.

"Yeah, she's not actually—"

"Oh, Dad, no. Please, no."

"What's wrong with Wendy from the DMV? How do you even know who that is?"

"She was at Career Day," Darius said in disgust. "Dad, all the kids at school talk about her. She's like super, super weird. She knits sweaters for her trees and stuff. She got kicked out of a city council meeting for getting everyone to sing a protest song. My reputation could not survive my dad dating Weird Wendy."

"What reputation?" Theo asked, feeling defensive. "Meeting her at Career Day doesn't mean you know her."

"I don't have to know her," Darius protested. "In a town chock full of odd people, she is the oddest one here. She's like the queen of kook. Please do not date an insane woman."

"I don't think she's insane," Theo protested. "She seemed really nice."

"Sure, serial killers seem really nice until they show you the basement!"

"I am definitely letting you watch too much television

out of your age range," Theo said. "Wendy is not a serial killer."

"That's what a serial killer would want you to think," Darius said direly.

"Darius, I really like her, and she helped me out with Jackson today."

"You don't owe her a date because she was nice."

"I don't owe her anything, I would just like to—" Theo was not sure how he'd gotten into the place of arguing with a twelve-year-old about a woman. "Darius, you said you don't have anything going on. Please watch Jackson for a few hours so that I can go out and be a normal adult human for a few hours. I'm not asking you to come on the date with me."

"What if I said no?" Darius asked dangerously. For the most part, he was a very reasonable and easy kid. He helped out when it was needed, and he was smart as a whip. He had terrible time management skills, but was usually cheerful and obedient. But every so often Theo saw his own stubbornness shine through, and he picked the damnedest things to stick on.

"Then I'll take Jackson with me and remember this the next time you ask me for that phone I've been thinking about giving you for your next birthday."

Darius, like any child, was bribable.

"Fine," he snapped. "But I'll remember this the next time you tell me my opinions matter to you."

Ouch.

The last thing Theo wanted was to drive a wedge between himself and his son. "Darius, I really appreciate your help. You've been amazing with Jackson, and I'm really grateful to have you on my team."

Darius had a look that suggested he wanted a fight, but he just hunched into his hoodie a little further and gave a suffering sigh before muttering, "Whatever," and fleeing to his room.

Theo wondered how he could have handled that better.

He's just a fledging, Theo's gryphon comforted him. *He'll get his flight feathers, eventually.*

Because that was just what Theo needed. A surly teenager that could *fly*.

CHAPTER 8

*W*endy arrived at The Miner's Grill at five minutes to six and was getting out of her car when Theo pulled up next to her in an older white pickup. She made a show of squishing herself against her car door and waved enthusiastically, then remembered that she was a grown-up and was probably supposed to have more decorum.

"I see you have temporary tags," she said, as they met at the backs of their respective vehicles. She tried not to fuss with her coat and wondered if she'd dressed correctly for a date. Theo appeared to have a collared shirt on under his winter coat and she'd gone deliberately casual, with a blouse that had cleavage, but not too much cleavage. She was wearing clompy boots with good soles, because heels in Montana in November were just dumb.

"A champion of a state worker was able to get them for me just yesterday," Theo said, sharing a knowing smile with her.

"Whatever would we do without competent state employees?" Wendy agreed. She was smiling absurdly at him, and she was pleased and gratified that his grin in return was just as silly.

"Probably we would have very unsafe roads," Theo said. "Shall we?" He offered his arm and Wendy shyly tucked a mittened hand into the crook of his elbow.

He gallantly held the door for her, and they were shown to a private table where they shed their coats. The restaurant wasn't fancy enough to have a coat check, so they were slung over the backs of their chairs. He was exactly as built as Wendy had suspected underneath his puffy coat. She sat down in her chair a little harder than she meant to and hoped that she wouldn't lose the last of her self-control and throw herself over the table at him. Those shoulders! That smile! She was smitten. He was wearing a dark blue collared shirt that might have been silk and he'd shaved touchably smooth.

Wendy wondered if she should have worn something that showed more cleavage.

"So, where in Nevada did you live?" Wendy asked, desperate not to let the silence get awkward and probably overcompensating by being too chatty.

"Las Vegas," Theo said, picking up his menu.

"Oh, were you a stripper?" Wendy asked before she could stop herself. "I mean, you could be. You have that hot bod and I cannot believe that I just said that, please don't look so appalled, and there's really nothing actually wrong with sex work, I don't want you to get the wrong idea here, I just thought it was funny until I heard it out loud."

"It is funny," Theo said, and to Wendy's relief, he did look like he was on the brink of laughter.

"Ah, so what made you move to fabulous Nickel City, Montana?" Wendy said, knowing that her cheeks were more flushed now than they'd been outside in the cold.

"Instinct," Theo said, and Wendy tried not to read too much into his curious expression. "And I had a job offer here, from a friend of a friend of a friend. I wanted a fresh start, and snow doesn't scare me."

"Oh, where do you work?" That was a normal thing to ask, Wendy thought.

"I wait tables at Larry's," Theo said. He still looked a little awkward, but he could probably not be faulted for being a little shell shocked. Wendy knew that she could be a lot and attempted to dial it in. "I was planning on getting a commercial driver's license over the summer because I'd like to work in construction driving big equipment, but Larry's kept offering me more hours and I never worked it in."

"Larry's is a nice restaurant," she said kindly. "Not that this isn't, of course! This is a great place, I can just see why you wouldn't bring me to a place you worked." At that moment, Wendy wasn't sure why anyone would go in public with her. She was like a barely trained circus monkey. "Are you ready to order?"

Theo did laugh then, a rich, warm laugh. "I'm looking at the steak and shrimp," he said. "But I'm thinking I'll ask what the special is."

A waitress hurried up, looking harried. "Can I start you with drinks?"

"Just water," Wendy said. "I don't need alcohol on top of my already questionable judgment."

"Iced tea," Theo said politely. "What's the special tonight?"

The waitress consulted her notepad. "A grilled lake trout served with rice pilaf and sauteed vegetables."

"Oh, that sounds good," Wendy said. "I'll take that."

"The surf and turf for me," Theo said. "Medium rare."

The waitress jotted both of them down and took their menus.

"I hope I didn't scare you off from the special," Wendy said. "Both cats and eagles like fish, so I expected you to go for that one, too."

To her relief, Theo got the joke. "My gryphon is sort of snobby about anything cooked, so I don't consult him much on dinner orders."

He *was* a gryphon.

"Tell me about yourself," Theo invited.

"Well, I work at the DMV," Wendy said. "Of course, you knew that!" She struggled for more to share.

"Do you have hobbies?"

It was a totally normal sort of question, but Wendy gave a little choke of laughter. "Oh goodness, do I. I knit. I crochet. I paint. I play piano. I sculpt. I have a weekend radio show on a fringe station. I terrorize my homeowners association. It would take less time to list what I don't do. What about you?"

"As a single dad, I haven't had time to really pursue anything. I'd like to learn to play an instrument someday."

Wendy thought that Theo playing a guitar—possibly shirtless—would be utterly devastating. "You said you had another kid. How old are they?"

"Darius is twelve," Theo said. He winced a little.

"Almost a teenager!" Wendy said. She snapped her fingers. "Darius R.! He's at Nickel City Middle School. I stamped his paper at Career Day last week."

"He…doesn't think I should be dating," Theo said reluctantly.

Wendy heard the unspoken *you* at the end of the sentence. "You mean he doesn't want you dating *me*."

Poor Theo looked like she'd put him in a spotlight

made of bees. There was no safe answer he could give as panic and dismay colored his expression.

Wendy took pity on him. "Nickel City isn't that big, and I'm sort of a community oddity. Little kids think I'm a witch and bigger kids think I'm just criminally uncool. Darius is probably right there at the cusp between the two."

"I think he'd like you if he got to know you," Theo said desperately. "He's just at a weird age."

Wendy cast about for a way to put him at ease again. "I remember middle school," she said kindly. "There is weird and there is what-the-hell-is-my-body-doing and also what are people and how is life?"

To Wendy's delight, Theo laughed, and didn't seem to think she was being too honest. "Yeah, I don't have awesome memories of that age, either."

"Did you grow up in Las Vegas?" Wendy asked.

That led to a laughing conversation about childhoods. He'd been a military brat, and she had grown up in a small community in Kansas with a large extended family. They both envied each other parts of their privilege—Wendy had always wanted to travel, and Theo had always craved more family.

"It's over-rated," Wendy said. "I had three sisters and a whole barrel of cousins. Everyone knew everyone's business and half the school had the last name Carmichael. I couldn't get away with anything."

"I don't know," Theo said. "I bet you got away with a lot. You seem like a ringleader."

Wendy gave a snort of laughter. "You aren't wrong," she admitted. "I was constantly leading the Carmichael kids into trouble."

"What brought you to Nickel City?"

I wanted to get away from a place where everyone knew I was defective, Wendy didn't say. Her entire extended family was made up of lynx shifters, and although they had never tried to make her feel bad for not being one, Wendy knew they had always wondered if there was something *wrong* with her. "Like I said, I wanted to travel, but I tried a couple of places and none of them really felt like home until here."

"Instinct?" Theo suggested.

"I don't have instinct," Wendy said, more sharply than she meant to. She tried to walk it back with a shrug and a careless smile. "I found a stable job, got a cute little house, and now I'm living the American dream!"

She was glad when the waitress brought their plates, and she could finally stop talking about herself. "Oh, that looks amazing!"

Theo cut into his steak. "It's perfect," he said with relish.

Wendy forgot to eat watching him take the first bite. That mouth! She still wasn't quite sure how she was here now with him. He seemed entirely out of her league and it felt a little surreal sitting across from him now, like it was all just a beautiful dream.

The ring of his phone cut into the fantasy, and Theo shot her an apologetic look and pulled it out of his coat pocket to check the screen.

His face blanched. "I'm sorry," he said, standing up abruptly and shoving the chair back. "I have to go *right now*. I'm *really* sorry." He snatched his coat from the back of his chair and fled for the door of the restaurant, leaving Wendy with a forkful of fish halfway to her mouth, frozen in surprise.

He nearly bowled over the waitress, who was bringing the iced tea she had forgotten.

Wendy was not oblivious to the stares she got. She put

her fork down and accepted Theo's iced tea for herself. "I'll probably need a to-go container for his," she said to the waitress as airily as she could manage. So much for going dutch.

After she had finished as much of the meal as she could stomach, Wendy paid the bill, put on her coat and wandered out into the parking lot with her bag of takeout. It was dark and the sky above was clear and full of stars. She'd seen the aurora once, on the northern horizon, and she always checked for them at night now.

There were too many parking lot lights to see them if they were there now, and Wendy thought about driving up to the Belle Lake Lookout. But that was a make out spot, and she had no one to make out with, so it probably wasn't worth the trip.

She was unlocking her car before she recognized what was bothering her, and she turned slowly to peer at the truck next to hers.

It was Theo's truck. Unless he'd driven away and a white pickup *exactly* like his had parked there.

That was possible, Wendy thought, but unlikely. And she couldn't think of any other explanation. Why would Theo leave her in the middle of a date, stick her with the bill for their dinner…and not actually drive away?

It occurred to her that maybe he'd had to fly. He was, after all, a gryphon. Was it faster to fly than to drive? Wendy doubted it. And wouldn't someone notice a great big gryphon in the sky?

She walked around to the back of the truck and looked at the plates.

Nevada. With the temporary tags that she had issued him the day before.

Where on earth had he gone?

CHAPTER 9

Theo stepped into Darius's room and let the slice he'd made through space close behind him. There was always a rush of silence at each end of the teleport, like it sucked up all the noise around him and he was momentarily deaf as he went through.

"—the hell is happening?" Darius shouted.

"Don't swear," Theo said, rubbing an ear. It was disorienting to be able to hear again after the complete lack of sound. Teleporting wasn't just like closing a door or turning off a stereo, it was like being dunked in a sensory deprivation tank. It came with splitting pain, but that was fortunately brief.

"Why didn't you tell me Jackson could teleport?" Darius yelled. He had Jackson in his arms now, bouncing him on one hip. The baby looked perfectly happy to have everyone's attention.

"I didn't know!" Theo protested. "Tell me what happened."

Darius sucked in a breath. "I put him into his crib in your room and he was squalling and squalling and I was about to go get him and then poof, he was falling onto my bed next to me and you gotta give a guy some warning about that, Dad, I nearly had a heart attack and if he can do that any time he wants, where the *hell* is he going to end up?" Darius had started out talking more quietly, but by the end, he was back up at full volume.

Theo reached for Jackson, who looked no worse for having successfully navigated his first teleport and squealed happily when Theo tossed him into the air and caught him. "He's just meeting all kinds of milestones, aren't you, kiddo."

Theo looked over in time to see Darius wince, and wished he hadn't said it quite like that. Darius didn't ever talk about it, but Theo knew he felt insecure because he wasn't a shifter. It must sting to have his baby brother already shifting and picking up obscure shifter magic on top of that.

"I honestly didn't know he would be able to do this," Theo said, moving to put an arm around Darius. Darius stepped just out of reach. "Not all gryphons can. Your grandmother can, but no one else in my family, and I wasn't doing it myself until I was seven or eight."

Darius blew out in disgust. "So, babysitting him is going to be impossible. He can just teleport himself into a candy machine or something?"

"There are limitations," Theo reminded him. He settled Jackson more comfortably on his shoulder and the baby gummed the collar of his shirt and tried to pull the buttons off.

"I know. It has to be to people you know."

"We were lucky he went to you, and not to me at the restaurant, or to Nevada with Juliette."

"I'm so flattered," Darius said sarcastically.

"You should be," Theo said firmly. "Teleportation works on trust. On connection. He knew you'd be safe."

"Part of instinct?" Darius snapped. "Great. One more thing I don't have."

"Darius, there is nothing wrong with you."

"There's not exactly anything right with me!" Darius countered. Sometimes, he was very grown up, and sometimes he was just a kid, with huge kid feelings, and none of the tools to deal with them. He'd just had a big scare, and Theo could guess how close he was to a complete meltdown.

"You want a grilled cheese sandwich?" he offered.

"I'm not a baby, Dad!" Darius snapped. Then he sagged in defeat. "Yeah, I do."

Jackson was pretty tired, and if he was like Theo, there was a fuzzy feeling following teleportation, like he'd just walked through cotton. He stopped trying to pull off Theo's buttons and settled in the crook of his arm, on the verge of sleep. Rather than risking putting him down and making him fuss, Theo made sandwiches for both of them one-handed.

"Sorry about your date," Darius said, not sounding very sorry.

Jackson started snoring.

Theo thought wistfully of the meal he'd left behind at the restaurant as he awkwardly put together two sandwiches and plates of chips. "Me, too. But hopefully we can try again sometime."

"I wish you wouldn't. You could do a lot better, Dad."

Theo looked at Darius in consternation and then turned back to the griddle, listening to the butter sizzle. Was this just a kid being a kid? Instinct said that Wendy was home, was the best path forward, and that their time was *now*. But he didn't want to push Darius away, and he'd already tested the poor boy's patience by bringing a shifter baby abruptly into their life at the worst possible time.

Surely, Wendy could wait?

Theo wasn't sure what was instinct at that moment, pushing him towards the vibrant woman with unwavering certainty, and what was just aching loneliness.

He wanted a partner, a helpmate. Theo couldn't lean on Darius for all of his companionship and emotional needs; he was supposed to be the *dad*, not the *dependent*, and sometimes Darius's dourness was like a lead weight that he didn't know how to lift. Wendy's laughter was like magic. He felt like a moth, and Wendy was a porch light at night; he was helplessly attracted and wanted nothing more than to bask in her gentle, happy brilliance.

Not that it was fair to her, drawing her into his tornado of chaos that was his life. His job was leaning on him to pick up more shifts, and now he had a shifter baby to juggle, and a surly older son who didn't want him dating Wendy, anyway. What did he have to offer her in return for all of his baggage?

She would get us, his gryphon pointed out with his infinite conceit.

I don't know if that's the prize you think it is, Theo answered wryly.

His gryphon puffed up in offense and sulked like Darius.

Well, at least the boy had inherited *something* from him.

After Jackson was down and Darius was dragging through his own nighttime routine, suddenly remembering that his wrist hurt, Theo tried to think of some kind of explanation to give Wendy that didn't give up one of the greatest secrets of his life and he recognized that he didn't want to make something up. He wanted to tell her the whole truth, and he had no idea how to do that. He was reaching for his phone to figure it out on the fly when he realized that he didn't have her phone number.

He didn't remember his truck until he went to take Darius to school the next day. He couldn't teleport in broad daylight, or fly to the restaurant as a gryphon, so he ended up taking them in a taxi and then he had to risk taking Jackson into school with him to sign Darius in tardy.

At least his truck didn't have a parking ticket on it when he got to it. Theo stared at the temporary tags until Jackson fussed, and then decided that his next task was to find Tiny Paws and see about day care for a teleporting, gryphon-shifting baby.

CHAPTER 10

"Nickel City DMV. Wendy's desk!"

Wendy answered the DMV phone without looking at the screen first and nearly dropped it when Theo's voice boomed out. "I'm really sorry I had to leave so abruptly," he said. "Really, really sorry."

"It's okay," Wendy said. "I enjoyed your leftovers for breakfast this morning."

Theo gave a surprised laugh. "Oh, good. I'm glad they didn't go to waste. And I'm really…I'm so sorry. Really."

"I've had worse dates," Wendy said honestly. At least he was *really* sorry. "I mean, at least you didn't leave with someone else." Or had he? That might explain why his truck was still there.

"Someone did that to you?" Theo said in outrage.

Theo probably hadn't left with someone else. Wendy was a pretty good read of character and he seemed too… upright. Like, if he wasn't interested in her, he wouldn't pretend to be.

Wendy felt like Theo was, for whatever reason, genuinely into her, but maybe her own libido was confusing her impression of him. She had never met anyone who set her alight like he did. She wasn't sure it wasn't just his pretty face, either. Yes, she'd teased him about being a stripper, with that gorgeous body, but it was really something in his eyes that attracted her most. Like there was magic there.

Of course, he was a gryphon, so there literally *was* magic there.

"It was a long time ago," Wendy said dismissively. "I got even."

Theo was silent for a moment and Wendy worried that it had sounded like a threat. She often came on stronger than she meant to. "Nothing that bad," she assured him. "I just put raw shrimp tails underneath the bucket seats of his Beamer. He had to sell it for parts six months later."

There was a noise on the phone, like Theo had nearly dropped it with a snort of laughter. "Remind me not to piss you off," he said.

"Don't piss me off," Wendy said flippantly. "There, I reminded you."

"I'm really—"

"*Really?*"

"—sorry."

Wendy had to laugh. "It's okay. Things happen." Wendy waited what she thought was an appropriate amount of time for him to offer to reschedule, or make it up to her with a hot booty call. Or even an explanation! When he didn't immediately have any of those things for her, she plowed on. "Don't forget to get that proof of residency and apply for your Montana license before your Nevada license expires. And your temporary tags are only good for two weeks."

"Oh, thanks," Theo said. "I'll do that."

"See you here," Wendy said dismissively. "We're closed between one and two for lunch."

"Oh. Great, thanks."

She hung up on him before she could drag out the conversation too long like a needy teenager, and spent the next half an hour going over what she'd said in her head. How long *had* she waited to let him offer to reschedule? It had felt like an eon, but she wasn't convinced of her own impartiality.

Finally, Wendy realized that she was spinning her wheels and looking wistfully at the phone—she didn't really expect him to call back, but she was really hoping—and shook herself. The day was wasting and surely she had something better to do than moon over some guy who'd vanished in the middle of a date and then called her at work with an unhelpful apology and no explanation.

No matter how hot he was.

CHAPTER 11

Saturday mornings were always pancakes, in part to coax Darius out of bed when he would otherwise sleep the day away.

Theo enjoyed cooking, when he had time for it, and he hummed as he mixed up the batter from scratch and set the table.

Jackson had slept in a little and was happily sitting on a colorful mat playing with an enrichment toy in the middle of the kitchen while Theo worked around him.

There was a grunt from the doorway and Darius appeared there, looking disheveled and sleepy.

"Good morning, sunshine," Theo teased him. "I made pancakes. They're almost ready!"

Jackson gave a cry of greeting and crawled to Darius, who lifted him up easily and swung him into the high chair.

Darius needed a haircut almost as badly as Theo did, and he sat down with his head cradled on his braced hand to shovel food into a body that didn't look like it absorbed any of the calories it took in.

Jackson had clearly never had pancakes before, and seemed to think they were for squashing flat rather than eating. He was quickly covered in sticky syrup.

"Did I tell you I have an appointment on Monday to take Jackson to day care?" Theo asked, sitting down to his own plate. "There's a place just for shifters here in Nickel City, and they have an opening for a baby."

"That's great," Darius said, like it wasn't.

"I'm getting my hours at Larry's switched over to a daytime schedule so that I can spend more time here in the evenings and weekends."

"That's great," Darius repeated with no interest.

"I'm looking at how much work it would be to get a CDL," Theo went on, pretending that Darius was holding up his end of the conversation. "An equipment operator would pay more and have better hours, with more advancement opportunities."

"That's great."

"I'm planning to run an excavator through your bedroom and hire a bucket of monkeys instead of doing anything for Christmas this year."

"That's grea—" Darius gave a little snort of laughter and then went back to his breakfast.

"Darius," Theo said more seriously. "I want to know what's going on at school. What happened that made you fall off the bleachers?" He'd been waiting for Darius to approach him first, but finally gave up on that happening and didn't want the incident to get too far behind them if it was something he needed to step in and handle.

"We were just screwing around," Darius said. "I lost my balance." He said it so sullenly that Theo knew that there had to be more to it than that.

"Were they harassing you?" Theo asked dangerously. He

knew that Darius hung around with shifters, even though he wasn't one himself, and Theo had no tolerance for bullying or hazing. Not that Darius would appreciate his *dad* riding in to the rescue. "Were they teasing? Did you get pushed?"

"It wasn't like that!" Darius said firmly. "I just *fell*!"

Theo wasn't sure whether to believe him or not, but let Darius eat in silence for a while. Was he trying to protect his friends?

"Dad?" Darius said hesitantly. "There is one thing..."

"Yeah?" Dad of the year award! Theo knew there was more to it.

"There was a doctor there," Darius said. "And he *did* something to me."

If Theo had been in gryphon form, he would have puffed up to twice his original size in agitation. As a human, he felt the hairs on the back of his neck stand up. "What did he do?" he asked.

"I think he *fixed* me," Darius said quietly. "I heard the bone snap when I landed. I heard it. I felt it. It was in a dozen pieces, I swear. I was sure that it was broken. I was positive."

"You were in shock," Theo said doubtfully.

"I'm serious, Dad. It was so wrong. And then that guy, that doctor, he held it and sort of *burned* into me while some mom blocked the view of everyone and I *felt* it all go back together. It hurt so bad, all those bones moving around inside the muscles. Like...I don't know...a peanut butter sandwich wrapped around a piece of broken celery."

Theo supposed he shouldn't be too worried for Darius if he could make an analogy about food. Everything about the twelve-year-old came back to food.

"Maybe it was just dislocated?" Theo proposed. "The

doctor might have just popped it back into place?" Could you dislocate a wrist like you could a shoulder?

Darius slumped in his seat. "I know what happened, Dad."

"I believe you," Theo said swiftly. "I do. It's…just a lot."

"Yeah." Darius sank back into sulky silence.

Theo chewed on this news. He really did believe Darius. It was probably no weirder or rarer than being able to teleport.

What was the convention? He couldn't exactly send a card saying *thank you for secretly healing my son,* even if he had any idea who it had been.

Wendy deserved an apology card.

Wendy.

Everything thought seemed to come back to her. Theo knew he had not covered himself in glory by leaving so abruptly, and he hadn't really explained what happened, or how he'd left without his truck.

She seemed to like him, but there was a whole wide world between *would bang that* and *willing to put up with the supernatural and mundane complications that this weirdo comes with.* If the tables were reversed, Theo was not sure he wouldn't have simply run away in the other direction. How much information did you trust someone with at this stage in a relationship?

He still didn't have her phone number, but he knew where she worked.

"Do you want to come with me to the DMV after school on Monday?" he asked Darius as they cleaned up breakfast together. Jackson was still in his high chair, sticking and unsticking his fingers together.

Darius's noise of disgust was answer enough, and Theo regretted framing it as a question or giving him an option.

"I want you to come with me and meet Wendy for yourself," he said more firmly.

"I already met her at Career Day," Darius muttered. "Crazy as a loon."

"I'm going to need more respect out of you," Theo said warningly.

"Why?" Darius demanded, slamming his plate down on the counter one-handed. "You're always going on about how respect needs to be earned and then you're sticking me with a baby to go out to an expensive dinner that we can't afford with a nutty woman that I don't want you dating!"

Jackson stopped playing with his fingers and stared at the two of them in consternation.

The rational part of Theo knew Darius had simply reached the end of his rope. They'd both had a rough, largely sleepless week with a needy new baby who could shift when he couldn't. Darius was probably in pain because of his wrist, whether it was broken or not, and now Theo was thinking about dating. It probably felt like he was losing his father altogether.

It was partly guilt and partly frustration that made Theo snap, "Don't take that snotty tone with me, young man!"

Jackson gave a little yelp and banged his hands on his tray.

"I'm not a young man!" Darius shouted.

"You're constantly asking me to treat you like an adult, but when it comes to taking responsibility, all of a sudden you want to be treated like a kid instead. You don't get to be what you want when it suits you!" Theo yelled back.

Jackson started crying.

"Don't talk to me about being unfair!" Darius had an expression of helpless rage as he shoved a kitchen chair out of his way with more strength than he realized he had. It crashed into the kitchen table and rattled all the glasses. "You don't even care about my life or what I need! Everyone else is more important and everything else happens first! I don't even matter to you!"

Ouch.

Theo felt like he'd been stabbed through the heart. He opened his mouth to protest that he was doing his best, because he was.

Then Jackson gave a shriek of protest and vanished right out of the high chair.

CHAPTER 12

*W*endy started her Saturday by getting up early and angry-painting on a huge canvas in the middle of her living room. She was just finding her groove when a tiny, sticky, shrieking gryphon popped out of thin air and fell into her palette.

"Jackson?!" Wendy added a few choice swear words that he hopefully wouldn't remember or repeat.

The stool that her palette balanced on was not equal to the baby gryphon's panicked struggle, and they both toppled over in a clatter of brushes, paint tubes, feathers, and scrabbling claws.

In a stroke of luck, the turpentine was in Wendy's other hand, so she was spared that extra disaster, but there was still plenty of chaos to go around.

"Not safe! Toxic! Oh, no! Don't put *anything* in your mouth!" Wendy hollered, trying to find a clear surface for her can of turpentine so that she could get Jackson safely up out of the paint without making things worse.

She balanced it precariously on a stack of books on an end table and scooped Jackson up with the palette. He clacked his beak at her and chirped as she tucked him under an arm and fled to the kitchen for paper towels. Jackson seemed to think that being toweled off was the most fun ever, and he shredded the towels and growled happily as Wendy got the worst of the paint off his fur and feathers.

"How are you so sticky?" Wendy wanted to know, taking him to the sink to finish the job. "Is that maple syrup? You smell like a greased-up Canadian."

Her heart rate was just starting to return to normal when there was another popping sound and Theo was stepping out of nothing at all and filling up her little kitchen with his big, magnetic presence.

"Most people call first!" Wendy shouted, more unsettled by his close proximity than his unorthodox arrival. "And use the front door! And how the hell did you do this? My house is *not* baby gryphon safe! It's barely adult human safe!"

Jackson was in the sink now and put his front claws up on the counter to give Theo a sheepish peep of greeting. Most of the color had come off with the paper towels, but it still looked like he'd been on the losing side of an argument with a rainbow.

Theo looked around in horror. "Wendy? Jackson? I'm...so sorry!"

Wendy wasn't sure if he was more scandalized by her messy house or Jack's colorful disaster, but she could only deal with one catastrophe at a time. "It's oil paint," she said matter-of-factly. "Let's get it off of him before he licks himself. Do gryphons have tongues?" Oh no, now she was thinking about Theo's tongue. "No honey, don't take that as a suggestion."

"What can I do?" Theo asked, sounding strangled.

"Keep him from getting loose or eating any of the

paint he's wearing," Wendy said. "The cadmiums are super toxic, and the cobalt is bad, too."

She started the water running in the sink beside him until the temperature was right—assuming lukewarm was even right for a gryphon—and then lathered up a generous handful of grease-cutting dish soap. "They use this on baby ducks after oil spills, so I have to assume it's safe for baby gryphons."

She soaped Jackson carefully, and Theo, standing close at her side, wiped the paint from his beak and helped rinse.

It was definitely a two-person job, keeping Jackson from trying to eat the colorful bubbles and getting the paint off of all the feathers and fur. He splashed and wriggled in joy.

Wendy got a stack of clean towels when he was finally rinsing clear, and Theo wrapped Jackson up and rocked him until he very abruptly fell asleep and shifted back into a baby boy.

Wendy didn't realize how much noise he'd been making—a constant soundtrack of clicks and squeaks and growls and chirps—until he was silent and limp in Theo's arms.

"I am so sorry," Theo said quietly, looking around.

"Really?" Wendy said sharply. She meant it to be funny, but she was still running high on adrenaline and flustered by Theo's nearness.

Wendy couldn't attribute much of the mess to Jackson's abrupt arrival. When she threw out the paper towels and rinsed off the paint palette, it wasn't much of an improvement. She righted the stool and put the caps on the paint tubes before getting the turpentine and taking it to the sink to clean her paintbrushes and store it more safely.

Theo tried to help, one-handed, until Wendy finally

told him, "Just stop. Go sit down over there and stay out of the way."

He sheepishly did, and the towel with Jackson in it gave a sigh of contentment and snuggled closer.

Theo was looking at her canvas. "That's beautiful."

"It's a work in progress," Wendy said uncomfortably. "Kind of like me."

Although she'd been angry when she started the painting, she never stayed angry long, and what had started as furious reds and slashes of oranges had resolved into an impressionistic sunset over an alpine lake, dreamy and fanciful, with rock spires and fluffy clouds.

"I really like it," Theo said. But he was looking at her, not the painting.

Now that the emergency was past, Wendy had questions, and she settled onto the stool facing him. It felt too bold to sit on the couch next to him, and that was the only other available seat. "So. You can *teleport*."

"And yes, Jackson can, too." Theo looked down at his tiny burden with wonder and dread. "That's why I had to leave in such a hurry, the other night. He scared the shi— he scared Darius."

Curiosity overcame Wendy's irritation. "Can you go *anywhere*? Do you have to have been there before? But neither of you have ever been to my house, so that can't be it. Is there a distance limitation? Can you take people *with* you? Is this why you left your truck at the restaurant?"

"It's specific to people," Theo explained patiently. "They act as an anchor. I can only go to someone I know *really well*, and distance matters, but not as much as you might think. It's really more about the strength of the personal bond."

It flattered Wendy that Jackson knew her well enough

to teleport to. But maybe babies really did bond that fast. "Will you need a ride home? I don't have a car seat."

"I've taken a person through with me before. It's a lot harder than a solo trip, but I should be able to take Jackson back this way because he's so little. I did not expect him to pick this up so early, or that he'd imprint on you. I think instinct plays a role, too, and kids seem to feel that more strongly than adults."

"I imagine having instinct as a shifter baby keeps you out of at least some trouble," Wendy agreed. "Jackson could have gone to worse places. Somehow. Do you want something to drink?" she offered impulsively. "I have juice and soda if you don't want to teleport home under the influence."

Theo chuckled. "Water would be great," he said.

"I could just wring out a sleeve in a glass for you," Wendy offered, realizing that the impromptu bath had gotten her and Theo as wet as Jackson. Theo's T-shirt stuck to him very nicely indeed. Wendy didn't want to think too hard about what bra she was wearing and whether it was visible through her damp blouse.

Theo chuckled and leaned back with Jackson in the crook of his arm as Wendy went to get glasses of tap water for both of them. Painting and scrubbing off gryphons was thirsty work.

Wendy had to get close to him to hand him the water anyway, so she got bold and sat beside him on the couch. There was a baby between them. What could happen?

"Thanks," he said gratefully, taking a sip. "I'm really…"

"If you say sorry again, I'm going to dump this glass of water in your lap," Wendy warned him.

"I think these are occasions that are worthy of apology," Theo protested. "But I will strike it from my vocabulary if it makes you uncomfortable. I just…I've been a terrific inconvenience to you so far."

Wendy had to shrug. "I mean, you certainly make life exciting. Maybe I've been stuck in a rut."

"I don't think there's a rut in this world that could hold you!" Theo laughed.

"Is that a compliment?" Wendy wanted to know.

Theo sobered. "I mean it as one," he said seriously. Then, just as Wendy was wondering if sitting next to him on the couch was a terrible mistake after all, he leaned over and kissed her.

$\mathcal{K}$issing Wendy was not the easiest thing in the world…and at the same time, it was.

Jackson nestled in the arm between them, so Theo had to lean to get to her mouth, careful not to crush the baby or jostle him awake, and not to spill the water in his other hand. He also wasn't sure what Wendy's reaction would be and had to be braced to draw back if he'd made the wrong call. Then his mouth was on hers and everything was exactly right.

There was a surge of instinct, that this was what he needed to do, and when, and underneath it, a tingle that was partly magic and partly passion. It wasn't just lust, though the sight and smell and warmth of her reminded him how long it had been since he'd been intimate with anyone but his own hand. He wanted to lay her down and bury himself inside of her, desperately and hungrily. But he also wanted to take it slow and savor the *anticipation* of her.

And more than any of that, he wanted to be here, with her, basking in her glow, feeling like everything in the world was right, even while his world was falling entirely into pieces.

She was just so…alive and full of energy. Theo couldn't understand why he hadn't thought she was his type when they met, because she was utterly gorgeous and everyone else he'd ever known paled in unfair comparison.

And now, the barest touch of her lips to his set him utterly on fire. He was enraptured, his entire world narrowed to her soft skin and the eager little noises she made as she opened her mouth and pressed against him.

He tried to gather her up, and forgot about Jackson, who gave a cry of protest at being squashed. He and Wendy startled apart. "Sorry, kid," Theo said, feeling more deeply sorry that he wasn't still kissing Wendy.

"I…don't really have a crib or anything," Wendy said breathlessly. Was she as enraptured as he was? Certainly her eyes were bright and dreamy, and she seemed to have trouble catching her breath.

"I should get back to Darius," Theo said regretfully. "I wasn't holding my phone when I came through, and he's probably wondering if I found Jackson and why I didn't come right back."

Darius.

Darius didn't want him seeing Wendy.

And he owed it to his kid—to both his kids!—to be a dad first.

"You're complicated," he said honestly. Jack had settled down again, snoring with his face pressed into Theo's shoulder.

"Says the man with the baby gryphon who just teleported into my paint," Wendy said sharply. "Don't you be calling *me* complicated, mister hot shot magical shifter."

Theo sputtered an apology, but Wendy put a finger on his lips. "I'm teasing. I know. I know how complicated *all* of this is, and you don't have to promise me rainbows and puppies. You…do whatever you have to, and maybe come kiss me later without a baby between us."

Maybe? Theo wanted nothing else in the world at that moment and he couldn't resist leaning in to kiss her one final time now.

He meant to keep it quick and chaste, but they both lingered over it, sharing air for a brief, blissful moment. Jackson stirred, and Theo finally tore himself away and stood up. "I'll figure it out," he swore. "I don't know how, but I will."

"Do I need to expect random baby gryphon drop-ins?" Wendy asked. "Should I get corner protectors and avoid using etching acids? Surround myself in bubble wrap in case he falls out of nowhere again? Oh, no, that's probably a suffocation hazard. Parenting is a minefield, isn't it?"

"You have no idea," Theo said. "Well, maybe you do, now." There was a streak of red paint on the carpet. "I should cover your cleaning bill. I wouldn't want you to lose your deposit."

"Oh, that's an old paint stain," Wendy scoffed. "And I own my house."

"Oh, and your towels…" Theo made a move to unwrap Jack, and the baby clutched them closer and screwed his eyes even tighter.

"Take them with you," Wendy said. "You can give them back later and Jack seems attached. Now I'm dying to see how you do this. Is there an incantation? Do you need holy water or herbs or something?"

Theo squirmed in embarrassment. "Nothing like that," he said. "I just have to think about who I'm going to and sort of…"

Unfortunately, he was thinking too fixedly about Wendy, and being glad that he had towels obscuring the front of his pants. His gryphon gave a burble of amusement. It was already much harder to teleport in human form; he felt like he had to focus as much on keeping his own shape as he did about his target.

Darius. He had to think about Darius and how much his son didn't want him seeing this fascinating woman, and how worried he must be. That amply quenched his libido, and after a moment of concentration, Theo could envision the twelve-year-old's skeptical date-ruining expression, feel his son's far-off presence, and tear open the space between them to step through.

He was not immune to Wendy's look of wonder, and he thought she might have said something as he slipped away, but the portal came with a rush of anti-sound, and he was deaf until it was closed again.

"—you finally find him?" Darius demanded. "Jeez, Dad, what took you so long? I was freaking out! I thought I might have to call Mom or the cops and I didn't have the foggiest idea what I was going to tell them because you said Mom didn't *know*."

The boy rushed forward, and, to Theo's surprise, voluntarily gathered Jackson into his arms. "You were probably pretty scared, kiddo. I'm really sorry I yelled."

Theo wryly thought that it was probably easier to apologize to a baby than it was to apologize to your father and accepted it anyway.

Jackson was more interested in going back to sleep and he grumbled and fussed until Darius tucked the towel more tightly around his kicking feet and rocked him gently. "Whose towels are these?" he asked skeptically. "Why is he wet? Was it…bad?"

"No, it was fine. I mean, he landed in a pile of paint and we had to clean him off, but it wasn't much worse than a colorful bubble bath. He seems fine."

"Juliette was painting?"

"No! It wasn't Juliette. I mean, your mom. He went to Wendy."

There was that libido-freezing, almost-teenaged look of disgust. "The DMV weirdo?"

"*Wendy*," Theo said firmly. "Apparently, she made a good impression on him."

"There is no accounting for taste," Darius scoffed. "I thought that at least Jackson had better sense. I'll put him to bed."

Theo watched Darius carry Jackson down the back hallway, shaking his head in wonder. Whatever complications had come with a second son, he was utterly awed by how well Darius had stepped up to the challenge. He might roll his eyes and complain the way only a kid could, but he was great with Jackson and was usually well-behaved. He stayed out of trouble in school and he was the best older brother Theo could possibly have asked for.

It could be a lot worse.

If only he liked Wendy.

CHAPTER 14

*W*endy slid into the diner bench seat next to her friend Dana and shrugged out of her coat. "How's the *puppy*?" she asked, after making sure they were out of earshot of the waitress and the other customers.

"You know how they are at that age!" Addison was sitting across the table from them. "Shifting is so new and exciting, and they just can't help themselves. We had to leave the grocery store with Gabby in a shopping bag last week."

"It could be worse," Wendy said, thinking about Jackson. She didn't volunteer details, though. It was discourteous to tell a shifter type without permission for normal animals, but mythical shifters were more secretive yet. Wendy hadn't even been sure gryphons *existed* until she saw baby Jackson.

"I imagine it was harder as a lynx," Dana said thoughtfully. "At least a wolf puppy can be passed off as a pet."

"Has Addison told you about her kindergarten

Halloween party?" Wendy asked, giving Addison a sly sideways look.

"Don't you dare!" Addison warned.

Dana grinned, looking between them. "This sounds like a story I would dearly like to know," she said cautiously, like she wasn't sure whose side to take.

When the waitress seated a party at the booth behind them, they switched their conversation to more mundane topics. Wendy waggled her eyebrows in promise at Dana, who giggled.

Wendy liked Dana, and it was nice having a friend in the shifter community who wasn't a shifter herself. Dana had only learned about it when her daughter shifted into a wolf puppy, so she was still very new to the hidden world. Wendy, on the other hand, had been the only one of her many siblings and cousins who wasn't a lynx shifter and had known about them—and was expected to be one— since she was a child.

But even though other shifters recognized her as one of them, Wendy had passed through childhood, then puberty, then adulthood, wishing in vain that she could be something she wasn't. No shifters could explain why instinct gave them that shifter tingle that was a false flag for her.

Dana and Addison ordered burgers and salads, while Wendy emphatically selected fries. "You guys can be virtuous or whatever. I'm not sharing."

"You said you had a date!" Addison remembered as the waitress gathered their menus and took their order to the kitchen. "How did it go?"

Wendy took a sip of her soda to give her time to consider her reply. *He had to leave and stick me with the bill when his baby boy learned how to teleport. Also, his older son hates me.* "Could have been better," she admitted.

"Was he a jerk?" Addison wanted to know, bristling

defensively. Wendy knew that Addison had dated her share of jerks in the single person of Owen Davis, and she knew what to watch out for.

"No!" Wendy said swiftly. "He was a total gentleman." *Except for leaving one bite into the meal and sticking me with the bill without an explanation.* "Really hot," she added, without meaning to.

"What's his name? Did he kiss you?" Addison said, perching her chin in both hands attentively.

Wendy wasn't sure how to answer that. He had, the following day, squashing Jack between them, but it wasn't really part of the date, so did she have to admit to it? "Theo. He had to leave early," she said dismissively, hoping that it sounded nonchalant enough.

"Why?" Addison prodded.

Wendy drank more soda.

"You can't start out like that and not give us more details," Dana scolded her.

"What was the problem?"

"Was he married?"

"She said he was a gentleman," Addison said to Dana. "A gentleman doesn't date around if he's married."

Dana shrugged. "Maybe he was one of those slick jerks who seems practically perfect but has like a basement dungeon or a string of wives in other states.

Wendy played with her straw and took another bracing sip of soda. "He was really nice," she assured them. "He's a single dad."

Dana and Addison nodded sagely and gave each other complicated glances. It would have been easy for them to have a contentious relationship, since Addison's newish boyfriend was the single dad of Dana's daughter Gabby. But they had both approached their friendship with open eyes and open hearts, and Wendy actually thought that the two of them were closer now than Wendy and Addison.

She tried not to feel like she was being cut out…of everything. She and Addison were cousins, not best friends. There was no reason to feel jealous.

"How old are his kids?" Addison asked.

"One is twelve, I think, and the other one is…I don't know, this old?" Wendy made Jackson's size between her hands. "Not really talking or walking yet, but definitely—," she trailed off in deference to the party in earshot. "I gave him the information for Tiny Paws, so I imagine you'll be seeing him on Monday to ask for a spot for Jackson." Of course, that had been before Jackson started teleporting. Wendy wasn't sure even Tiny Paws would accept a baby that could portal around at will.

Addison's face lit up. She absolutely loved kids, and Wendy was not sure there was anyone in the world more suited for working at a day care for shifters. She was gentle and tirelessly patient and sweet.

Unlike Wendy, who lived in a house that was full of toxic art supplies and sharp implements. She didn't know a thing about kids—preteens or babies.

"Is the older one a boy or girl?" Addison wanted to know. "Are they…one…too?"

Wendy shook her head. "Theo said he wasn't." Though he *had* been hanging out with shifters at school.

The waitress brought their burgers and Wendy was glad that the subject turned to safer topics. Even if they hadn't been talking about shifter complications, she wasn't particularly comfortable talking about what she and Theo had. Or didn't have, really.

He'd kissed her, but he hadn't mentioned another date. Wendy told herself that was probably because he had kids taking understandable priority in his life, and not because he didn't want to date her. He had talked about kissing her again.

She was so distracted thinking about Theo, his rakish smile, his tousled hair, his graceful stride, that she didn't notice Addison stealing her French fries until the third one. "Hey!"

"You weren't here!" Addison laughed, stuffing it in her mouth. "Mooning over, what's his name—Theo? Is it short for Theodore? Is he a big stuffed bear?"

She and Dana speculated about his shift type in code and Wendy blithely ignored them and ate her burger.

"How's Tiny Paws doing?" Wendy asked, when she'd given up defending her fries from Addison and traded them for the cherry tomatoes from her salad.

"We've got a waitlist!" Addison said happily. "If you know anyone who might want to work there, send them our way. Your new boyfriend should get in, we've got an opening for another baby. It's just the older kids that we have to chase."

"He's not my boyfriend," Wendy insisted. "We don't even have a second date." It didn't count as a second date if his kid dropped out of thin air into a palette of paint and then he kissed her on her couch.

"Veronica still sniffing around the day care?" Dana asked, lowering her voice. Veronica was the nightmare owner of the day care property and she kept threatening to raise the rent or sell out from underneath Cherry, who ran the day care.

Addison sobered. "We caught her coming around after hours last week—I wouldn't have known if I hadn't gone back for my phone. And we found a camera set up looking into the backyard. We took it down and destroyed the memory card and it hasn't been replaced."

"A camera?!" Wendy was horrified. A camera at a day care for shifters was a terrible risk.

"She was trying to surveil the day care?" Dana sputtered. "Does she…*know?*"

"I don't think so," Addison said. "She tried to spring a new contract on Cherry that forbade pets, and it seemed a little…peculiar. I mean, I thought it was just that she has this bizarre vendetta against Cherry and is looking for any reason to evict her."

Cherry kept a small zoo of pets at the day care to act as deflection in case one of the young shifters was caught in the wrong form. It might not save their secrets if it was a rare shifter like the little Chinese unicorn who was there with her baby brother, but the snowy owl baby, Amy, had been passed off as a chicken more than once by putting her in a cage while she was sleeping.

"I've been keeping an eye on the local neighborhood chats," Dana offered. "A couple of neighbors saw a lion in Tails last week. People jump in and scoff about it, but chatter is kind of high right now."

"Any photos?" Addison asked.

"Thankfully, only really blurry ones."

"Olivia says Veronica was asking her specifically if she'd ever seen any weird wildlife around, and suggested she might pay for photos, if she did," Addison said thoughtfully.

"Ugh," Wendy said. "That woman needs a hobby. She's been just awful since the city council kiboshed her shady short-term rental business."

"Let's talk about something more pleasant," Addison begged.

"You said you had book news," Dana reminded Addison. "Did you get an agent?"

"Oh! I have two of them who responded to my

proposal. They think they can get a deal with a big publishing house!" Addison, for all that she pretended to be grown-up and serious now, still bounced in place like a child. "I've got copies of their contracts to look over!"

"That's amazing!" Wendy really was happy for her. Addison deserved a lucky break, and the picture book she'd written for one of her students really was a sweet piece of work. Roderick, her boyfriend, had done illustrations for it, and Wendy was not at all jealous that Addison was on her way to a book deal, despite the fact that Wendy had wanted to be a writer for a large portion of her life and had seven novels within a chapter of being finished. Addison's book was even illustrated, and Wendy didn't feel bad that Addison hadn't thought to ask her own cousin about illustrating it.

Of course, it made sense that she'd ask her boyfriend to do it, even though Roderick wasn't really pursuing a career as an artist and made a perfectly good living as a plumber.

Addison deserved the boyfriend, too, and Roderick was a great guy, protective and kind and funny, and his little girl *adored* Addison and there was no preteen in the picture glowering in her direction and making his dad choose between them.

Okay, maybe Wendy *was* a little jealous. But she was absolutely not going to let Addison know that. "Isn't Olivia talking about opening up a little art store downtown on the same block as Tiny Paws? Maybe you can do a book signing there!"

"That is so far off," Addison said, but she said it with a dreamy, hopeful look in her eyes that Wendy knew from the inside.

At some point, Wendy had stopped having those dreams. She had accepted that nothing she tried was ever quite good enough.

CHAPTER 15

*J*ack was a baby—a *human* baby—and Theo was concentrating hard on that small blessing as he stood outside the day care. "Stay like this," he murmured. "Please stay like this a little longer."

Tiny Paws didn't look like a day care from the outside. It looked like an attempt at a historical gold rush saloon, even though Nickel City had actually been part of a much later and more modern mining boom. A cheerful, hand-written sign said "Ring for Tiny Paws!" next to a button and a camera.

Theo dutifully rang.

"Come on in, Mr. Royal!"

Theo had his arms full of baby and diaper bag and applications, and he'd called ahead for an appointment. He opened the door with an elbow when it buzzed and brought a swirling cloud of cold air with him when he went in. There was a long, narrow entranceway lined with cubbies and hooks, most of them hung with tiny coats. A small chaos of boots and mittens and hats cluttered the bench and floor, and a rather alarming cartoon bear warned him to take off his shoes. A whole wall was covered with mismatched socks on pins and a block print note asking parents to please check for lost items before they left.

Theo had to dodge several puddles of melted snow after he slipped off his boots, and he was watching where he stepped so carefully that he missed the approach of a young woman at the gate back into the day care.

"You must be Jackson and Mr. Royal."

"Theo," he said with a sigh of relief. They were off the street, safe from prying eyes, and this woman was definitely a shifter. "And this is Jackson."

"Hi, Theo and Jackson."

She had the same strawberry blonde hair as Wendy, and there was something about her voice and her grin full of mischief that was very familiar. "Are you Addison?"

"Indeed," she said drolly. "Wendy's cousin, Addison."

"I brought the application," he said. "And here's my ID."

"Gosh, no wonder Wendy likes you," Addison teased. "She's a sucker for anyone who has their paperwork in order."

Theo tried not to take *Wendy likes you* too seriously, but he felt his heart lift. *Did* she like him? She'd kissed him like she liked him, but Theo had been out of the dating pool so long, he wasn't sure how any of it worked anymore. And this felt different. It wasn't just flirting; his heart and his gryphon were also tangled up in it.

Instinct said she was *right*.

But Theo worried he was just mistaking *right now* for *right forever*, and it scared him how much he longed for *right forever*.

Addison had given up waiting for him to come up with a clever response because he was still caught up on *Wendy likes you,* and she invited him into the day care. "Come on back and meet Cherry. She's just finishing up with a story."

To Theo's surprise, Cherry was not a shifter. There wasn't even the tiniest tingle of magic from her.

The rest of the room was a different story. Theo had never seen so many different baby shifters in one place. His experience was that shifter families kept their children close and secret until they weren't a danger. They probably looked old-fashioned from the outside, like women were expected to stay home with little ones, but he knew as many fathers who had done it as mothers. It could be a financial hardship. But then, so could day care. Theo was going to have to look carefully at the budget and adjust his work schedule to match their hours.

This reminded him that he should follow up with Juliette about child support and official custody paperwork. He'd been so busy trying to keep up with Darius and Jackson and his heart that he'd forgotten to wonder about Juliette's secrets.

Jackson was staring around in interest as Cherry finished her story, though Theo wasn't sure if he realized that most of the children listening to her were shifters. Juliette had enrolled him in a regular day care in Las Vegas. Did Jackson even remember it?

"Baabaah abbaha!" he exclaimed, pointing at a mirror.

"It's you!" Theo whispered. "It's you!" He bounced him in place as Cherry shut her book and released the children out into a happy chaos of play.

"You must be Theodore Royal," Cherry said, rising easily from the floor to offer her hand. She looked both young and old, with steel gray hair tipped in blue. Her smile reminded Theo of Wendy; it had the same flavor of mischief.

"Theo is fine," he said, shaking her hand. Still no magical tingle of shifter recognition.

"And this must be Jackson."

Jackson got suddenly shy and turned to hide his face in Theo's chest, clinging harder.

"He's sometimes shy," Theo said apologetically, though he figured Cherry knew that most babies were. "He's also sometimes, a, ah, gryphon." Now *he* sounded shy. But it had been enforced since he was a child of Jackson's age that he wasn't supposed to talk about being a gryphon.

Cherry took that completely in stride. "That's a new one for Tiny Paws," she said cheerfully. "Are there any particular needs that he has?"

Theo licked his lips nervously. "He sometimes teleports."

He felt some pride in making Cherry do a double take. "That is also a new one for Tiny Paws. Is there something we can do to contain him? Anything in particular that triggers it?" She looked serene after her moment of startle.

"It's only happened twice now," Theo said, leaving aside the fact that it had been twice in three days and very recently. "I'm hopeful he'll be distracted enough here to want to stay. If he does teleport, it should be to me, or to his big brother Darius, or to Wendy, who works at the DMV. His mom is in Nevada, which is probably too far away."

"We're all about keeping the kids happy and entertained," Cherry said. Theo could see that she was dying to ask questions and trying to stick to what she specifically needed to know. "What kind of protocol do we need to follow if it does happen? How can we keep him safe?"

Theo found himself liking her questions and her common sense. She clearly understood both shifters and children, and it wasn't long before Jackson had given up being shy and was grabbing for Cherry's wiggling fingers.

"I'm really sorry to be extra trouble," Theo said, belatedly remembering Wendy's admonishment not to apologize so much.

Cherry didn't threaten to drop a drink in his lap. "We have a two-year-old who can shift into a squirrel and breathe fire. We'll manage."

"We're in?"

Theo hadn't realized how tense he was about the whole affair until Cherry nodded. "Welcome to Tiny Paws!"

CHAPTER 16

*W*endy told herself that the zing of excitement she got when she saw Theo and Darius come into the DMV lobby and take a place in line on Monday afternoon was just libido. It wasn't a Hallmark movie moment, and there wasn't actually a swelling sound-track when she caught sight of the gorgeous guy with the car seat and his scowling son.

Well, there *was* music, but it was just the 80s station, playing *Shot Through the Heart* for the seventh maddening time that day.

It wasn't true love, Wendy scolded herself, turning her attention to hurrying her current customer through their form. And if it was, she didn't have instinct to tell her about it. "If you could just take that to the next window and fill it out while I help the next person, that would be great. Here's a pen. I'll call you right over when they're done. You're not losing your place, I promise."

The old woman, looking skeptical, shuffled aside with her purse and her paperwork and Wendy called the next person up. "Oh. Mr. Charles Vissey Smith. Did you get your glasses prescription updated?"

"Ophthalmologists are a racket," Mr. Charles Vissey Smith grumbled. "It'll be two weeks before my new glasses get here, but you said I could get a restricted license, so I'm here for that."

"Can't you just wait the two weeks?" Wendy asked. "Those have to be approved by the district supervisor in Butte, and it's going to take almost as long to get that done as it is to wait for the glasses."

"Got stuff to do," Mr. Charles Vissey Smith said gruffly. "Ain't going to let them oppress me."

"Did you print the forms online?" Wendy said with faint hope.

"I pay my taxes like everyone else," the old man said acidly. "You can print a few pages for me."

"Let me get you those forms," Wendy said with resignation. Was it worth having to deal with him another time if she gave him an incomplete packet and made him make another trip? No, it really wasn't. She printed the form and the supplemental form and the justification sheet.

"Can you step aside and fill those out?" she said hopefully. "There are people waiting." *Really gorgeous people.*

"I waited my turn!" he protested. "They can wait their turn."

Wendy accepted the forms from the woman who had been gracious enough to go to the next counter and promised her, "I'll give you a call when the plates are in."

Mr. Charles Vissey Smith dotted all his i's and crossed all his t's and grumbled through the entire process. "Make it hard and hope we'll all just give up," he complained, passing the form over to Wendy at last.

"I'll call you when I get the approval," Wendy said with

false cheer. "Or the denial, of course. It's out of my hands!"

She was gazing past him at Theo and Darius and Jack. Theo caught her eye and grinned in greeting. Was it a slightly sappy grin? Wendy was positive hers was.

Mr. Charles Vissey Smith muttered something about government workers doing too many drugs and stomped away at last, leaving the lobby empty except for Theo and his kids.

Darius refused to look in her direction and had that patented not-a-teenager-but-desperate-to-be air of practiced nonchalance as they approached the counter. Theo was smiling so wide that Wendy could have counted his teeth. She'd really like to be counting his teeth with her tongue about then.

"Proof of residence!" he said, waving a bill. "With my street address, not just the post office box."

It wasn't true love, Wendy reminded herself again. It was just…hormones. No one had kissed her in a really long time, and now that someone had, her body was revved up and ready to go. "That'll do fine then," she said. "Your application is already in the system. We just need to take a photo and I can print your card. Hi, Darius."

Darius made a noise that was halfway between polite acknowledgement and rude brush off. Theo frowned at him in warning. "Darius, this is *Wendy*."

"We've met, Dad," Darius said, hunching into his coat.

"Career Day," Wendy said with amusement. "Are you still sore because I didn't have chocolate at my table?"

"Oh, I heard all about that." Theo looked back at Darius. "We should pick up a learner's manual while we're here. You can apply for a permit soon."

"Not for like two years, and it's all online, Dad," Darius groaned. "I don't have to be here."

"Well, I appreciate the help," Theo said with more than enough charm to make up for him. "Thanks, *Wendy*."

Darius rolled his eyes. Wendy tried to catch his gaze for an understanding grin and failed. She glanced back to see that Theo had seen her attempt, and he had a sappy half smile on his own face.

Jackson chose that moment to scrunch up his own face, concentrate hard, and then burst out crying.

"Dude!" Darius said, waving a hand in front of his face.

"I'm going to go change Jackson," Theo said, grimacing. "Can you stay here with the car seat, Darius?"

Darius gave a groan of protest, but Theo swiftly strode away. He didn't seem the slightest bit abashed at carrying a pastel diaper bag or bouncing a fussy Jackson on his hip.

That left Darius with Wendy. "I can give you a print copy of that learner's manual if you want to get started learning the road rules," she offered.

"Gee, thanks," Darius said sarcastically. He seemed to hear himself. "Sorry. That would be great."

Wendy found one and passed it over the counter. "Look," she said hesitantly. "I really like your dad, but I don't want to make it weird for you." She paused, hoping he would say something helpful like, *That's okay*, or *You're not weird*. When he didn't, she bulldozed on. "I'm not saying we'd ever be best buds or anything, but I'd like to get along."

His face did about seven different things, all of them disgusted or skeptical. Finally, he took the manual. "Thanks," he mumbled. "Whatever." He cast a desperate look at the exit.

"So. What's your favorite subject in school?" Wendy tried.

Darius shrugged.

"English? Economics? Math? Recess?"

"There's no recess in middle school," Darius scoffed.

Wendy blew out in frustration. "Throw me a bone, kid. You think that trying to make friends with some moody, self-absorbed, prepubescent twerp who hates me sounds like fun?"

Darius gave a surprised shout of laughter, which is what Wendy had been hoping for, and he shot her most of a smile before he smothered it in outrage. "Tell my dad I went to wait in the truck with the car seat," he said. He slung the car seat effortlessly off the counter with his braced hand and sauntered out with his other hand in his coat pocket, his hood pulled over his face.

Theo was back with Jackson shortly after. "Darius?" he said, looking around in concern.

"Waiting in the truck. I am too uncool to hang out with more than"—Wendy made a show of checking her wrist—"one minute and sixteen seconds."

"I'm—" He stopped himself.

"Good job!" Wendy praised him. "Now, let's go get your glamor shot, Mr. Royal, and you can have a shiny new license before you leave."

He put Jackson on the floor with a toy, and Wendy sat Theo down at the photo booth. "You've got some hat hair going on," she warned him. "I'm not sure where our mirror went. Someone didn't put it back where it belongs."

Theo did a terrible job trying to blindly smooth it.

"No, you're missing the worst bit. Over to the left and back a little. No, *your* left!"

"You don't have a mirror in your purse?"

Wendy snorted. "Do I look even a little like someone who has a mirror in my purse? Here, let me do that." She told herself to keep it professional, but it felt a little like time stopped having meaning when her fingers touched his soft hair and she was honestly not sure how long she spent trying to tuck his unruly dark locks into order.

Stop petting the gryphon, she told herself, forcing herself to back away at last. "Now you won't embarrass Montana," she said breathlessly. "This isn't a passport, so you're allowed to smile, but you have to keep your mouth closed and look at the little red dot above the camera and think of cheese or whatever."

She snapped a series of photos and picked the best of them, trying not to linger too longingly over the lines of his face. She sent it to the license printer with the efficiency of much practice and in a few minutes, had a warm license to pass across the counter to him.

"Thank you," he said. "Not a bad shot, I think."

"I'm not sure you could take a bad shot," Wendy said, knowing that she sounded absurdly twitterpated.

"Darius is waiting in the car," Theo said. Jackson was lying on his back kicking, but in Wendy's unlearned estimation, he was not really fussing as much as he was just experimenting with his legs.

"Don't want to keep him waiting," Wendy said wryly. The reminder of Darius's dislike was a pretty good dampener on their conversation.

"Thanks for all your help," Theo said.

But he didn't offer to take her out again and Wendy wasn't going to bring it up first.

He picked up Jackson and backed halfway out of the lobby, then finally turned around to watch where he was going after he'd run into the stanchion that was supposed to keep crowds queued up neatly.

CHAPTER 17

"Good morning Mr. Royal!" Addison sang at him. "Good morning, Jackson!"

Jackson gave a squawk of outrage or greeting and flapped and kicked against the car seat cover. Theo really hoped he got his shifting more under control before warmer weather came to Nickel City, because the car seat cover was the only thing keeping their secret right now. At least this had all happened in November, and not in June.

"I'm really—" Theo bit back his apology. He hadn't realized how much he did it until Wendy pointed out. Of course, he'd had a lot to apologize to her in particular for. "Jackson seems to be in a mood this morning. And you can call me Theo."

"That's what we're here for, Theo," Addison said merrily. She accepted Jackson over the baby gate that separated the entrance from the private back room of the day care. "Have you seen Wendy lately?"

Subtlety apparently ran in the Carmichael family.

"I got a Montana driver's license on Monday," Theo said. "My plates are on order."

Addison, bouncing Jackson in her arms with care for the sharp bitey parts, raised a skeptical eyebrow at him and chewed on her lower lip. Finally, she blurted, "Look, I didn't mean at the DMV. I know Wendy can be a lot. But you should…give her a chance."

"Wendy is great!" Theo said swiftly. "I'd like to see her again! I would! I just, I mean, between Jackson and Darius and work, it's been complicated."

Addison grinned. "Oh, that's wonderful! I just think you guys would be great together! If you want me to babysit Jackson some night so you can go out, just say the word!"

Jackson bounced in Addison's arms, clacking his beak and trying to scramble up to Addison's shoulder. She deftly flipped him onto his back in her arms, ruffling the fur on his belly and folding his wings around him like a blanket. He started purring, his eyes half-closed.

Theo took mental notes.

"Her birthday's coming up next week," Addison said suggestively.

Give her a gift! Theo's gryphon said firmly. He was surprisingly materialistic for a creature with almost no grasp of the concept of money and frequently urged Theo to give tokens of their affection. He insisted on thoughtful gifts for every occasion and was almost childishly giddy about birthdays and Christmas.

I don't know if we're to the point of giving birthday gifts, Theo objected.

Birthday suit means naked, Theo's gryphon announced unhelpfully.

"What does she like?" Theo asked out loud, trying to drown on the images that his gryphon was fixating on.

"Like for a present?"

Theo realized belatedly that Addison had been trying to angle him towards asking her out to dinner. He opened his mouth to apologize for misunderstanding her and closed it again without speaking.

"Wendy's pretty easy to shop for," Addison said. "I just buy her the weirdest things I can find and she loves them."

"Would she want art supplies?" Theo guessed. "She paints really well."

"That would be harder to get right," Addison cautioned. "She's kind of particular about quality and knows exactly what she wants." She gave Theo an astonished look. "Did she actually *show* you her paintings? She doesn't usually do that."

"I caught her working on one," Theo said, though really, *Jackson* had caught her working on one. By teleporting straight into her palette. "She's really good."

"She's so good," Addison gushed. "Wendy would never tell you, but she got scholarship offers to three colleges for art that she didn't take. She writes, too, and draws, and sculpts."

Somehow, that didn't surprise Theo. "She seems amazing," he said, knowing he sounded completely besotted. "Isn't her talent sort of wasted at the DMV?"

"Everyone says so," Addison agreed, gently redirecting Jackson's chewing to a toy she found in one of her pockets. "She says it's because an art or writing career is too unpredictable and doesn't come with health care. But I think it's because of what she *isn't.*"

"A shifter."

"She's never said that it bothers her," Addison said thoughtfully. "I don't know if it does. She seems made of self-confidence and independence, but I sometimes wonder if she thinks there's something wrong with her because out of her whole extended family, she was the only one who never shifted."

"Why concentrate on the one thing you can't do?"

"Human nature?" Addison proposed. "Maybe it's conditioning? At some point, being proud of your work is considered childish. You stop hanging work on the refrigerator and start hiding it in closets. Maybe she got a really tough critique of her art at some point and it broke her spirit. I don't know!"

The front door chimed and Addison checked her phone one-handed and let another parent into the lobby.

"Thank you," Theo said, keenly aware that they were having a highly personal conversation about a woman he barely knew and was already half in love with. He gave Jackson a last tickle. "Have a good day."

Jackson clacked his beak and purred.

Theo walked out into the biting wind and blowing snow and wracked his head for an appropriate gift.

The only things that came to mind were the very *inappropriate* gifts that he wanted to give her, and his gryphon was no help, suggesting that they steal her a museum or commission a gold-plated statue of her.

CHAPTER 18

Wendy didn't need any more problems. She already had plenty of problems in her pants. She definitely didn't need to be dealing with Veronica Chase.

"These are the forms I'll need you to fill out to transfer vehicle ownership from your personal name to a business," Wendy said patiently. "They're each going to cost the same amount. No, there is not a bulk discount I can give you."

"This is supposed to be a money-saving move," Veronica groused. "I don't understand why everything costs so *much*. It's still my own fleet!"

"That's just how it works!" Wendy said, as cheerfully as she could manage. "I don't make the rules, I just stamp the licenses!"

Veronica muttered something cutting under her breath about how state employees were clearly overpaid as she snatched up the forms and took her carefully made-up self away.

Next in line was Mr. Charles Vissey Smith.

Again.

But to Wendy's surprise, he didn't storm up to her workstation with unreasonable demands. He caught Veronica's arm, and when Wendy expected the woman to shake him off impatiently, they instead stepped aside and had a quiet conversation while the next person in line came up to get a license renewal form.

Veronica and Mr. Charles Vissey Smith were still talking when Wendy was finished with her customer, and she heaved a sigh of relief when they left together.

Wendy was approving online forms, marking incomplete replies—how hard was it to get all five digits in a zip code? And shouldn't the form be able to check for something that basic?—when she finally realized what was bothering her about the exchange she'd witnessed.

Wendy was great with patterns. Art, music, math…it was all patterns. She didn't have a lot of training or technique, but she knew what came next, and how to predict the notes in a melody or the place to put a pleasing element in a painting. She looked at the world and saw how trees and leaves worked, what made one garden perfect and another *too* perfect.

And Veronica Chase was starting to fall into a pattern that worried Wendy.

It wasn't just that she was an unethical landlord who was more interested in lining her pockets than providing people with *homes*, it was that she was getting suspicious.

Wendy thought about motivations, all the little gaps and inconsistencies in Addison's story. Why would Veronica have something against Cherry, of all people? Cherry was the sweetest, most selfless person that Wendy had ever met. It wasn't like there was anyone else vying to rent the Tiny Paws property. So if money wasn't the goal, and a general vendetta was highly unlikely, why else would Veronica be so interested in the day care?

Wendy thought better with something in her hands, and she started doodling aimlessly on a sticky pad with a ballpoint pen as she answered the phone and updated someone's personal information in her database.

It had surprised Wendy to see her talking to Mr. Charles Vissey Smith. What were the chances that they had something in common? Mr. Charles Vissey Smith was all about freedoms and conspiracies, his whole life an effort to find someone to blame for his failures. Veronica was about exploiting systems for her own personal gain.

Conspiracies. Personal gain.

Certainly, Mr. Charles Vissey Smith had a few wild conjectures that weren't so far from the actual truth. But the rest of his worldview was so unhinged that no one who wasn't just as misguided would actually listen to him. Wendy didn't think anyone would take his ravings about *shapeshifters* seriously.

Unless Veronica had suspicions about *shifters* and was looking for someone to validate them.

Veronica, for all her other faults, was clever. She might put the facts she found together. She'd told Olivia that she was interested in photos of local and exotic wildlife she might see. By itself, that was a harmless request. But when Wendy paired that with her attempts to surveil Tiny Paws, a dangerous picture started to come together.

Veronica Chase either knew, or strongly suspected, that there were secret shifters living in Nickel City. What would she do with that information if she had it? How would it serve her best? Would she sell it to the highest bidder? Try to monetize the secret? Blackmail?

She'd need evidence for blackmail to work, and conjecture wouldn't get her far. Who would she tell about shifters if she did have such evidence? The press? It would take more than blurry security footage and hearsay to do a major reveal, and what would that *gain* her?

There was a picture emerging from Wendy's doodles, and she realized she was drawing Theo like a besotted teenager. With a sigh, she tore off the top paper and dropped it into the wastebasket under her desk.

The phone rang, and Wendy knew just before she answered that it was Theo. "Nickel City DMV. How can I help you?" *Out of your pants*, she hoped.

"Hi, Wendy," he said, so haltingly that Wendy had to pause and rewind the conversation in her head to make sure that she hadn't added the part about pants out loud. "Theo here. I wanted to thank you for your help this weekend. I didn't, properly. Before. And I owe you for dinner, still."

"Is this DMV business?" she asked. "I should give you my personal number."

"It's not, I mean, I'd like that. I…it had just been a few days and I didn't want you to think I wasn't still thinking about you, and this was the only way I knew to reach you. Oh. I probably could have asked Addison."

Was he still thinking about that awkward kiss with a sleeping baby between them? Wendy certainly was.

The silence grew stilted and Wendy cast about for something to say that was properly encouraging and not entirely flinging herself at his feet. "We should try again for that dinner some time," she suggested.

"Yes!" Theo said eagerly. "Absolutely! I'd love that!" But he didn't offer a date or a place, and he seemed to hesitate then. "I could ask Addison to babysit, because…"

Darius. Darius still didn't like her and Theo was clearly conflicted by his son's dislike, not to mention unable to lean on him for childcare.

Wendy couldn't really blame the boy. She was a lot to

take, even for grown-ups, and she remembered how tricky that age could be trying to balance popularity and puberty. The last thing he needed was a wacky woman dating his dad. He was already dealing with a surprise new baby brother and his life—even more than Theo's—was really complicated right now.

"We'll have to do something sometime," Wendy said breezily, not wanting to pressure Theo into anything. "Something that doesn't involve emergency body paint removal. Oh, sorry, I've got a customer coming in. I'll talk to you later! Bye!"

Wendy wasn't sure if she was glad for the old woman coming in or mad at the interruption. She'd never been good with phone calls where she couldn't see people, but that had been an uncomfortable conversation, to say the least. She really did think that Theo was interested in her, which was both surprising and flattering and extremely mutual, but that wasn't the same as willing to sacrifice his relationship with his kids and Wendy couldn't imagine asking him to.

It wasn't until after she'd hung up that she realized she had forgotten to give him her number again.

CHAPTER 19

Switching his work schedule to the hours that Tiny Paws was open and Darius was in school did free up more time for Theo to spend with his kids, but it meant a lot less money. The lunch crowd wasn't as likely to have multiple drinks and tipped far less generously.

It also meant a lot more randy housewives, who were much grabbier when they weren't out with their husbands.

"Save me," he begged Laura, when he retreated for the kitchen feeling flirted out. "I'm running out of ways to say 'I'm not interested in being your boy toy' without risking my tips. I had to tell them the specials five times because they were giggling so loud."

"They asked for one of your tables specifically," Laura said with a shrug and a laugh. "Not my fault they think you're cute."

Laura was as gay as it was possible to get, so her assessment of his cuteness was completely non-threatening. She was herself ridiculously cute and exactly as charming as she thought a customer deserved. She took a tray, shook her head at him, and went out to serve a tourist family with a child who was running laps around their table, to the danger of everyone in tripping range.

Theo refilled drinks around the restaurant and returned to smile winningly at the table of flirtatious older women and take their orders.

When he brought their orders to their table later, he passed Laura going into the kitchen, and was alarmed when she winked at him.

He lay down each plate with panache more due a fancy dinner than a simple lunch, giving each woman a moment of attention and a special smile before he moved on. They didn't flirt back, to his surprise, and when they left, their tip was a relief. "What did you do?" he asked Laura suspiciously. "Did you make promises I can't keep?"

"I told them about Jackson," Laura said matter-of-factly. "I said you had to work double shifts to support a secret baby your mean ex had hidden from you."

Theo groaned. "It wasn't a secret baby. I knew about the baby. And Juliette's not…mean. We're just not good together."

"Yeah, but that's not as good a story."

"Laura!"

Laura made up more and more outrageous stories for each new table, and Theo got through his shift and gave Laura a portion of his tips. "You more than earned this," he told her, as they settled the register before the dinner shift started.

"Go home to your poor secret baby and your Cinderella son, Prince Eric," Laura said, accepting the tips as her due.

"I think you're mixing up your fairy tales," Theo said dryly.

"As long as there's a happy ever after, who cares about the details?" Laura laughed.

Darius cared about the details when Theo broached the idea of dating Wendy again over dinner.

"And I guess it's up to me to babysit, like always," Darius groused.

"Her cousin Addison from the day care offered to watch him. I could have her come over and keep an eye on you both."

Darius bristled. "I'm *twelve*, Dad! I don't need a babysitter!"

"Then you can babysit Jackson yourself. You don't get to play it both ways."

"I *don't* like her."

"Well, at least she's trying to like you," Theo said in despair. "You're not even giving her a chance."

"Look, it's not like I have any choice in this. I never have any choice."

"What choice do you want?" Theo asked, not quite able to keep the frustration out of his voice. "Do you want to pick a different girlfriend for me? Do you want me to live out my life like a monk? Do you want me to stay just-friends when I finally feel like maybe this is something that could work out for me? I'm not asking you to call her *mom*! I just want you to be more friendly so she doesn't think you're a complete jerk and I'm a crappy dad."

"I'm sorry I make your dating life so difficult!" Darius shouted.

Jackson gave a warning cry and banged his spoon on the high chair.

Theo and Darius both quieted.

That last thing they needed was for Jackson to teleport. Would he go back to Wendy's again, or would he pick Cherry or Addison now that he'd been at Tiny Paws for a few days? There was no way to predict it.

Jackson gave a grunt of satisfaction and returned to

chasing peas and pieces of broccoli around his tray with fingers that wouldn't do exactly what he wanted.

Darius ate his dinner, because even when he was mad, he was a growing boy who would vacuum up anything put in front of him and ask for seconds.

Theo left him to his sullen silence and kept his conversation pointed at Jackson, offering him bits of his own dinner when the peas and broccoli lost their appeal.

"Look," Theo said, just as Darius started to say, "Dad-"

"Ablababla!" Jackson said.

"If you want to date the kooky shifter chick from the DMV, I guess I can't stop you."

"How big of you," Theo said dryly. "But she's not a shifter."

Darius wrinkled his face in that skeptical you're-wrong expression that he constantly wore. "You said you knew she was safe to show Jackson to."

Theo returned to his own meal. "Yeah, but that was mostly instinct. She's like you, just gives off that feeling, even though she's not actually a shifter. I guess it's more common than I realized."

He looked up to find that Darius was staring at him, his fork suspended mid-air. "You didn't think that was important to tell me?"

Theo shook his head, trying to remember their conversation in detail. "I thought I did tell you. And I mean, half the shifters I meet, I don't *actually* know for sure if they're really shifters. It's impolite to talk about it, not to mention dangerous. Maybe a lot of them aren't."

"I would have liked to have known that!" Darius insisted.

"I'm pretty sure I tried to tell you," Theo said, picking up the spoon that Jackson flung to the floor. "Does it matter?"

To his dismay, Darius stood up, shoving his chair back. "You don't know what matters to me! And you never tell me anything!" he hollered, and then he was stomping from the room.

Theo heard his bedroom door slam, and Jackson chortled and banged on his high chair tray.

"Puberty is awesome," Theo said to the baby with a sigh. "So, you've got that to look forward to."

CHAPTER 20

Wendy woke to a Saturday with a sky of falling snow and made herself get out of bed, even though it was the last thing she wanted to do.

She found no solace in any of her projects. She just wanted to get lost in something for a while, find that groove of creativity that made the rest of the world go away and ride a burst of inspiration to a final product.

But nothing kept her attention long. She kept circling back to remembering Theo's kiss, wondering what it would be like in Theo's arms…in Theo's pants. She threw the paintbrush down into the can with a clatter. The painting wasn't working. She felt frustrated and pent up and discouraged. She was good at everything, but not good enough at anything, and it was all useless and her house was small and cluttered and she ought to just donate everything to charity and start over entirely.

She was never going to amount to anything. She was the crazy lady who worked at the DMV. The one that the neighborhood committee kept having to correct. There was nothing in the rules about knitting on trees until

Wendy had done her yard project, and then, of course, everything had to be amended and she was going to have to unravel three skeins worth of worsted wool from her birch trees if the resolution finally passed. Practically the only good thing about Veronica Chase buying up the property in the area is that she single-handedly meant the committee didn't always have a forum to approve changes.

Wendy was always the problem. If she had a warning label, it would be: Prone to making unpredictable but enlivening choices.

She washed the paintbrushes, because as much as she just wanted to pitch everything into the trash, she never left paint in brushes. She always cleaned up and put things away when she was done, and treated her tools with respect.

Her house didn't look like a hoarder lived there because she was untidy. She just had too many ideas. She had so many things that she wanted to do, and none of them ever went anywhere in the end. Maybe she should just give up on thinking that she would ever make anything important. She was just never going to be as good as her vision, and there was no point in any of it.

She worked at DMV for job security and health insurance, not for fulfillment, and her ambition outstripped her ability at every turn.

Most of the time, Wendy was happy with her choices. She had a good job and owned her own house and didn't have a family to eat into her hobby time. She could afford to buy art supplies and do crafts according to her whim; she didn't have to try to turn everything into a hustle like so many artists.

It was the smart choice. The sensible way to live her life.

But sometimes Wendy felt like she was letting go of a

part of her soul, and she didn't know which part it was, or how to hold on to it.

She put the paints away and folded up the easel. The painting could go in the spare room to dry where she didn't have to look at it, leaned up against the piano she rarely played.

It had finally stopped snowing, and there was a blanket of white snow across her front yard and driveway. Maybe something more physical would clear her mind. Wendy slipped on her winter boots and a coat, and trudged out into the crisp air. The homeowners association would complain if she didn't clear her sidewalks, and it would be smart to be able to get the car out if she needed it.

She hadn't gotten very far before she looked up to find a familiar figure watching her from the half-cleared street.

"Hi, Darius," she said. "What are you doing way over here?" She knew from Theo's paperwork that they lived several blocks away.

He shrugged and didn't answer.

"I've got another shovel leaning against the side of the house if you want to help," Wendy said.

Darius waved his braced wrist at her.

"How long are you going to use that as an excuse?" she asked. She might not have instinct, but she knew a crutch when she saw one. "That's a brace, not a cast or an amputation. You didn't have any trouble slinging the car seat around at the DMV."

"You think I'm a slacker now?"

Zing! She'd hit a nerve. She knew his type. He was willing to coast a little, because people expected him to, but he would never find it truly fulfilling. He needed stimulation. Challenge. Novelty.

"It's okay," Wendy said with a theatrical shrug. "I'm sure you couldn't keep up with me anyway."

"But you're old," Darius blurted. "It wouldn't be a fair race." He seemed to realize how rude it would sound only after the words left his lips.

Wendy feigned fiery offense. "Oh my god, you skinny little whippersnapper. Go get that shovel and prove yourself on the battlefield of my driveway!"

Darius scrambled to do so, but his backwards glance was full of laughter.

They squared off on opposite sides of the driveway. "We each have to do half the driveway and the section of sidewalk to the corner of the property," Wendy declared. "The first to finish gets all the glory and bragging rights."

"That's lame!" Darius said. "We should make it worthwhile."

"Fine," Wendy countered. "What do you want to wager?"

"Five bucks?" Darius suggested.

"You win, I'll give you *ten* bucks. I win, you let me date your dad," Wendy countered.

That drew Darius up. "You wouldn't date my dad if I won?"

"I might still do it, you can just be a jerk about it if you want," Wendy scoffed. "I've even already done some of your sidewalk, so you've got a head start to make up for being so young and worthless. Go!"

"Young and what?!"

Wendy took advantage of his outrage to start in on her sidewalk, shoveling furiously.

"You can't shovel into the road!" she warned over her shoulder. "They'll fine me for that!"

Darius flung a load of snow into her yard, hitting one of the yarn wrapped trees. It stuck to the fibers, adding a surreal new layer to the art piece.

Wendy decided she liked it, and then she was too busy shoveling for a win that mattered.

She shed her hat first, then her scarf joined the yard knittery, and by the time they met in the center of the driveway, she had her coat open and was panting and sweating. To her relief, Darius looked as tired as she was, and he wasn't wearing his coat at all.

"You tricked me," he said, leaning on his shovel and breathing hard. "You gave me the part of the driveway where the snow fell off the roof and made a big berm."

Wendy shrugged out of her coat and went to collect her hat and scarf. "I really wanted to win the bet," she said. "Anyway, age and wisdom will always win."

"Are you trying to teach me to cheat?"

"I'm teaching you to use your brain before your body," Wendy said. "You want some hot chocolate, or are you too cool for that?"

Darius shrugged. "I guess."

He stared around at the inside of her house when she led him inside. "Dude, you're weirder than I thought. What is *that*?"

"It's a sculpture."

"Is it…a six-foot octopus made of yarn and car parts?"

"It's art. It can be anything you want. How's your wrist?"

Darius looked at his wrist like he'd forgotten he had one. "A little sore," he admitted. "That's more than I've done with it in a long time."

"You want an ibuprofen or something? You're twelve, right? Can twelve-year-olds have those?"

"I'm twelve," he confirmed. "I don't need anything."

He wandered around the house while Wendy made hot chocolate—good hot chocolate from milk and cocoa powder. "Probably I shouldn't offer you a shot of whiskey in this," she said.

"Probably shouldn't," Darius agreed, with a snort of laughter. "You're a good painter. Did you make this quilt, too?"

Wendy brought him a cup of the cocoa. "I can add more sugar if you want," she offered. "Or whipped cream, if you need it fru-fru."

Darius accepted the cup. "Nah. Thanks. This is good." Then he took a sip. "Oh, this is *actually* good!"

"Never say it's good before you've tried it. No one will trust your word."

Darius looked at her thoughtfully.

"Make a show of trying it, and then lie through your teeth about how good it is," Wendy added.

"Teaching me to cheat *and* lie," Darius observed.

"You'll have to catch my lessons on stealing and deceiving next week," Wendy said.

"You're not really good with kids, are you?"

"I've never tried before," Wendy said quietly. She didn't want to tell Darius that she had never wanted children. How would that feel, that she wouldn't want him in her life? She was also startled to find that she actually did. He was a good kid, smart and steadfast, and if he wanted to protect his reputation, it was hard to blame him for that. Now that he wasn't doing the sullen, pouty *I hate you* routine with her, Wendy thought he was actually interesting, which was not a word she had ever considered applying to someone so naïve and unformed, and she might even come to like him.

"Why aren't you a shifter?" Darius asked.

"Do you know about recessive and dominant genes?"

"I mean, why do you feel like one? Dad says…it's like I

feel. Like other shifters think I am one, even though I'm not."

Wendy waited for the pang of doubt and disappointment that she always felt at the reminder, and found that it was far more muted than usual. Maybe misery really did love company. "I don't know," she said. "I remember spending a lot of time wondering what was wrong with me, why I wasn't what I should be."

"How do you get over it?" Darius asked. Oh, there was the nearly-teen angst, in spades.

"Do you?" Wendy asked him frankly. "I'm not sure it's a thing you get over. It's just a part of the bigger mosaic of you, and if you spend all your time thinking about that one thing, that's all you are. You shape yourself by choosing what to think about. So, if you don't want to be caught up in something you can't actually change, stop dwelling on it."

Darius blinked at her.

"I read that on one of those inspirational posters they put up at work," Wendy admitted. "The DMV is a real drag, and they have a bunch of that kind of crap in the break room for employee morale."

Darius was in the middle of taking another sip of his hot cocoa and choked on it as he burst into laughter that turned into coughing as he held in his mouthful of cocoa until he was red in the face and tears were leaking from his eyes.

"You almost killed me," he told her, when he could speak again.

He drained the cup with the exuberance of someone who hadn't learned how to savor. "Well, thanks for the chocolate," he said, licking around the rim. "And the exercise."

"Thanks for helping me clear my snow," Wendy said.

Darius put his coat on and wrestled his sleeve over his brace. "I guess you can date my dad," he said, grudgingly.

"I did cheat," she reminded him.

Darius gave her a hint of a smile. "Yeah. But he likes you. And I can see why."

"I like him, too," Wendy said seriously.

Darius fussed over his buttons. "Maybe you could come over for dinner sometime."

Did he want to supervise the date? Did he plan to sabotage it? Wendy thought he looked like he already regretted the idea.

He added, "But could you…not kiss? Like ever, where I can see it?"

"That wasn't part of the bet," Wendy said.

CHAPTER 21

"I can't believe this was Darius's idea," Theo said, as he opened the door for Wendy on Monday night. He still hadn't remembered to get her phone number, so he'd had to wait until the DMV was open again to call her. "Whatever you did to him, bottle it." He had to gaze at her in delight for a moment. Her cheeks were pink with cold or excitement, and her eyes were sparkling.

"I badgered him into shoveling my sidewalk with a wrist brace, cheated on a bet, and taught him how to lie," Wendy said with a wry smile. "I'm a terrible influence and you should never allow me around children, ever."

Theo had no choice but to laugh. "C'mon in."

If she had dressed up for the occasion, it was hard to tell as she took off her coat. She was wearing a broomstick skirt and a tight-laced shirt. There might have been makeup around her eyes, and her lips were kissably red, but she was also biting them, so that might be why. If she had styled her hair, it was ruined by the warm hat she pulled off and was now in a halo of static around her face.

"Your house is…lovely."

Theo looked around at it doubtfully. It wasn't an ugly house, but it was…very austere. He'd never gotten around to putting up artwork or hanging photos. There were a few bookshelves that showed some character, but compared to Wendy's house, it was a hotel: unlived-in and barren. Jackson's toys in one corner were all that cluttered the place, and there weren't even that many of those. He'd only been there for two weeks, Theo realized in astonishment, even though it felt like a lifetime already. He hadn't had time to buy much for the boy.

"You're too kind," he said. "And I mean that. This place is where beige goes to die."

"That sounds like Darius," Wendy observed.

"I think he said it first," Theo said. "He's got some posters up in his bedroom, at least."

Theo's brain got stuck on the word bedroom, and he had to wonder lustfully if he was going to get to take Wendy to his own bedroom, and if anything could possibly happen with his on-site two person chaperone team. He was happy to have her companionship for the evening, but his body was reminding him how much *more* there could be.

There was a cry from the hallway, and Jackson came crawling out to greet Wendy. Darius followed just behind him, looking ready to save him from careening into a wall or sticking a finger in an outlet.

"Look at you motoring around like a little disaster waiting to happen," Wendy said to Jack. She glanced at Darius, then looked at Theo. "Any teleporting recently?"

Theo gave a sigh as Jackson did a cheerful faceplant into the carpet and Darius helped him back up on all fours. "No, and I'm hoping he's forgotten how to do it altogether. Plenty of shifting, and that's hard enough."

"How's Tiny Paws working out?"

"I don't know how I would survive without it. It's been a lifesaver. He loves it there and comes home tired. He's even slept through a few nights."

"Bliss!" Wendy said.

"Can we eat?" Darius suggested. "I'm starving."

"You're always starving," Theo said, moving into the kitchen. "I made baked chicken thighs and mushroom risotto."

Wendy clapped her hands. "No wonder it smells so amazing in here. You didn't tell me you cooked!"

"You were expecting takeout?"

"Honestly, yes. Or something from a box."

"I threw out the box before you got here," Theo joked. "No, I made it from scratch. It's not that hard."

"You'll have to teach me," Wendy said. "Darius, pay attention. Girls love a guy who can cook."

Darius looked appalled.

"Or guys," Wendy said. "I wouldn't judge."

"Girls!" Darius said swiftly. "Definitely girls."

"Either way is fine," Theo assured him.

"Girls!" Darius squawked, looking mortified.

"How many chicken thighs do you want?" Theo asked, bending to take them out of the oven. "Are you hungry?"

"I'll start with one," Wendy said, as he set them on the stovetop. "Those look amazing!"

"They'll have to cool for a moment," Theo warned. "Two for you, Darius?"

"Three, please!"

Darius joked with Theo about his bottomless stomach as he loaded the plates. "It's my bag of holding!" Theo was relieved that the boy seemed willing to banter with Wendy around, not just clam up and refuse to be social. She really was a miracle, and he caught himself smiling and nervous every time they were close.

It was a giddy *falling* feeling, Theo realized. He was utterly losing his heart to this woman, and he was glad to have Jackson and Darius there and part of it, because it wasn't just Wendy that he wanted, it was this *family*. She was a gear in their machine that Theo hadn't recognized was missing and after only a few moments of joking in the kitchen, he couldn't imagine not having her there.

There were only two chairs that matched the kitchen table, and Theo and Darius jostled good-naturedly over who would take a wobbly stool. Darius won by playing the young-and-flexible card, and Theo pretended to limp around the kitchen with a cane.

There was no eating baked chicken with utensils, so they all literally rolled up their sleeves and dug in. The meal was boisterous and cheerful. Jackson seemed to wear as much as he ate, and he was a constant source of entertainment, frequently grabbing his food and then failing to notice when he dropped it. Wendy laughed until there were tears in her eyes watching him search his fingers for what he'd just lost. Everything was even funnier with Wendy to laugh about it with.

She licked her fingers after finishing her chicken and Theo caught himself gazing at her raptly.

She caught him. "As long as I'm not the least mannered person at the table, I figure I'm doing fine," she said teasingly. She pretended to eat her napkin.

Darius snorted with laughter and nearly dropped his chicken in his lap.

endy wondered if all preteens were this mercurial.

One moment, Darius was laughing with them at the dinner table, the next he was sulking over some imagined insult. The next, he was flouncing to wash dishes…and then…

"Do you want to see my animals?"

Most of the time, Darius acted above his age, in Wendy's uneducated estimation. He was bright and articulate. At this moment, she remembered he was still a child, and he looked very young and uncertain.

"Animals? Plural?"

Theo was wrestling the tray of the high chair off and promising Jackson a cookie if he stayed in place. "He's got a whole zoo in his room," he warned.

Stronger women than Wendy would have melted at Darius's shy invitation. "Yeah, I'd love to."

She followed Darius, now sulky and silent again because apparently that wasn't the right answer, either. Wendy was never going to figure kids out.

They were greeted by the wee-wee alarm of a guinea pig and a symphony of little noises that included the hum of motors, the buzz of lights, and a chorus of cricket chirps. Wendy stared around in awe. "It really is a zoo!"

For the amount of chaos, it was all very well contained, and while there was a scent of sawdust and animal to the room, it wasn't overwhelming. Every cage was clean and homey…and there were a lot of cages.

"This is impressive," Wendy said. "Some kids just collect bottle caps."

"No kids collect bottle caps," Darius scoffed.

A tiny bird in a hanging cage chirped and hopped from perch to perch as it sang. There was a snake in a tank, basking under a hot light, and a lizard in another tank below him on a log. "That's a bearded dragon," Darius offered, when Wendy bent to peer at him. The tank below that looked empty.

"Crickets," Darius said.

The guinea pig was purring now, and it came to the door of the cage to sniff Wendy's fingers.

"You want to hold a chinchilla?" Darius offered, shy again.

"Oh, yeah!" Wendy didn't have to feign her enthusiasm.

"Do you have any pets?" Darius asked, opening the cage. The chinchilla looked like a mouse crossed with a rabbit, and it squeaked and climbed into Darius's hand willingly.

"Not right now," Wendy said. "I used to have a cat, but decided not to get another when she died so that it was easier to travel." Not that she had actually traveled, once she had the opportunity.

Darius passed her the little creature. It was denser than she expected, and incredibly soft.

"That is the softest thing I've ever touched," Wendy admitted. "I can see why they make coats out of these."

Darius snorted because he was too cool to actually laugh. Wendy asked him questions about the animals, and he proved to be more than slightly knowledgeable.

"You thinking about growing up to be a vet?" she asked him.

"I'm thinking about it," Darius said. Then he seemed to realize he was being too eager and quickly added, "Maybe I'll be a ballerina."

Wendy shouted with laughter, and Darius looked startled and uncomfortable.

"Thanks for showing me your animals," she said honestly, figuring her tour was over.

"Whatever," he answered.

Wendy wasn't sure why her first glimpse of Theo again should affect her so strongly. She had just had dinner across from the man, and watched him play goofy games to get peas into a fussy baby who could teleport away from things he didn't like.

But every time Wendy saw Theo after being apart for even a moment, it was like seeing him for the first time all over again. He had lost none of his movie star handsomeness, even after being flung with disdained peas, and Wendy couldn't understand why he felt so dear, or how she could be so hot for him.

"You weren't kidding about the zoo," Wendy said, hoping she didn't sound too breathless. "It was cool. Do kids still say cool?"

"I can't keep up," Theo admitted with a chuckle.

"I should get home," Wendy said, feeling shy herself. "You've got kids to get to bed."

"Hey!" Darius protested. "I'm not a kid."

"You're a kid," Theo said firmly. "And you've got school tomorrow."

"Darius asked me not to smooch you in front of him," Wendy whispered to Theo as she got her coat and scarf off the hook by the door. He held her coat for her to slip her arms into, very gentlemanly.

"Let me walk you to the porch," Theo said, just as quietly.

The door wasn't quite shut behind him before he was scooping Wendy into his arms and she was lifting onto her toes to put her lips on his. She'd worried that she'd built up their first kiss too much in her mind, that she'd added too much fantasy to her memory of it. But this was twice as hot, with no baby to be careful of between them.

Any intentions she'd had of keeping things slow vanished. Wendy pressed herself wantonly up against the hard length of him, and twined her fingers in his hair—he desperately needed a haircut and Wendy hoped he never got one—and he held onto her like a drowning man as they kissed and kissed and kissed.

Her ears got cold and her fingers went numb, or Wendy would have kept making out with him on the porch much longer than she did. When they broke apart, their breath steamed in the cold like dragon smoke and Wendy felt like her lips were on fire.

Theo licked his own lips and Wendy was ready to brave frostbite to take off her clothes for him right there on the porch, when there was a wail of outrage from inside and Darius cried, "Dad!"

"Duty calls," Theo said regretfully.

"Better not let it go to voicemail," Wendy agreed, every bit as regretfully. "Thanks for dinner."

"Thanks," Theo echoed.

Then he was slipping away from her to go inside of his

house and Wendy had to hold herself back from flinging herself at the door and begging him to let her in.

She stood there a while longer, straining for the sounds of Theo's low voice, too muffled to make out words, and Darius's higher response, and Jackson's shrill laughter. It was warm in there, warm and full of love, and Wendy had never wanted to be a part of something so much in her entire life.

Not to mention, that terrible, tantalizing man had wound her up to a level of frustration that Wendy couldn't remember. She yanked her hood up over her ears and stuffed her hands in her pocket. It was going to be a long, cold, lonely night in her big, cold, lonely bed.

CHAPTER 23

"I'm sorry to call you at work, but I still owe you a dinner," Theo said, before he remembered that Wendy had told him to quit apologizing for everything.

"You owe me a lot more than that," Wendy said. "Can you please hold for a moment?"

Theo spent his time on hold listening to the tinny, too-loud music and fretting that she really was mad at him.

"I had a client who needed his hand held through some forms," Wendy said cheerfully as she came back onto the line. "Didn't you already feed me dinner?"

"I wasn't sure a basic dinner at home with my kids was equal to sticking you with the bill for a meal out! I feel obligated to make this up to you."

"That's what every little girl dreams of," Wendy teased. "To get asked on a date out of *obligation!*"

At least, Theo hoped she was teasing. "I'm sorry—"

"I don't have a glass of water to dump in your lap, but I could probably find one."

Theo had to laugh. "Fine! I would really like to take

you out again some time and it's not just an obligation, and I would love to make it more but I'm having trouble finding a sitter because Addison offered but she wasn't available this week and Darius has some evening thing for the school play, so can I at least see you for lunch?"

"You sure it's not an obligation?" Wendy said archly.

"I'm positive," Theo assured her. "Tomorrow is my day off at Larry's and I'd like to buy you a sandwich at Heads Up and maybe smooch you while Darius is in school."

"Oh, smooching!" Wendy exclaimed. "I'm in. I'm off between one and two. I'll meet you there."

Unfortunately, it turned out that smooching was not actually all that easy to do. Theo very badly wanted to kiss her, especially when her cheeks were all flushed from the cold and she was shaking snow off her hood. But the bakery was crowded, and it didn't seem appropriate to make out while they were waiting in line, so Theo settled for standing very close to her and making nonsensical conversation about the weather and the decor.

"Are you together?" the cashier asked, as they placed their orders at the counter.

"Yes," Theo said, delighted that the cashier might think they were together...just as Wendy said, "No."

"This is my treat," he insisted.

To Theo's delight, she got very flustered, which was something that he hadn't realized she could even do. "Sorry, I forgot. I'm used to paying my own way."

"No need to apologize," Theo said, handing over his credit card. He had to smile at Wendy, who was studiously looking at the takeout menu that she'd already ordered from.

Confident, no-nonsense Wendy was amazing, but Wendy looking unexpectedly shy and nervous was absolutely *adorable*.

They got a tiny table in a noisy corner under a heater that made them both shed several layers. Wendy was wearing a tight purple blouse with a chunky necklace of purple crystal and black cut glass beads wrapped in silver wire.

"I like your necklace," Theo said, when he'd finally gotten his coat wrapped around his chair and managed to sit in the narrow space left by the crowded tables.

"Thanks," Wendy said with a genuine smile, reaching up to toy with it. "I made it in a metalsmithing class I took at the local college."

Their conversation started with the usual topics, but it was Wendy, so within a few bites of their sandwich, they were comparing the weirdest foods they'd ever eaten. "Crickets, probably," Wendy said. "I don't recommend them. They're kind of uncomfortably crunchy and have odd limbs that stick in your teeth."

"Okay, I'm eating a sandwich with sprouts, and now I am thinking about cricket legs sticking in my teeth. So, thank you for that."

"I'd apologize," Wendy said slyly. "But we're not doing that and I'm honestly not sorry to make you uncomfortable for a change."

Theo snorted in amusement. "What did I ever do to you?"

"Looking all movie star good and flirting with me in public until I can't even make complete sentences, for starters. Are you sure you weren't a stripper in Vegas?"

Theo glanced sheepishly around the bakery and changed the subject back to safer topics, like eating bugs. Wendy let him get away with the dodge, but Theo was sure she had noticed.

"What's next?" Wendy asked when Theo had finished his sandwich.

"Dessert?" Theo asked in confusion. She still had half a sandwich left.

"No, I meant, with us. Are we lunch buddies now? We've had zero complete dates and two really hot kisses, and I have to say that kind of confuses me."

"I think you're pretty amazing," Theo said, loving her honesty and wanting to reflect it. "And…I'd really like us to be more than lunch buddies."

Wendy looked away first, looking flustered again and more than a little pleased. "I like the idea," she said. "But I know the logistics are a little complicated."

His logistics, Theo knew. Between Jackson, who was a massive shift risk, and Darius, who was a little black cloud of doom, he came with a lot of baggage. Every second of his schedule was blocked out for being *dad*. It wasn't really fair to Wendy to try to make a relationship out of this.

But he'd never wanted anything quite so badly, or felt instinct pressing quite so hard. Wendy was his happiness. He wasn't sure how to work her into his existing life, but he knew she belonged there.

"Wendy…"

She looked up and what she saw in his face must have been clear, even if Theo himself wasn't sure what it would be. He wanted her, in a simple carnal way. She was pretty and lively and he kept imagining what it would feel like to hold her down on the bed beneath him and make passionate love to her. He could still taste her stolen kisses and remember the feel of her up against him when they'd made out on his porch. He wondered what those clever fingers would feel like on his skin, twined in his hair, what it would be like to bury himself in her and make her beg for him.

"I think I'm going to get the rest of this sandwich to

go," Wendy said. "I've got about fifteen minutes before I have to be back at the office."

"We could drive up to the Belle Lake Lookout," Theo suggested. He hadn't lived in Nickel City for very long, but long enough to know that it was a popular make out point for young people.

Wendy's eyes danced and her smile made dimples appear in her cheeks. "What a lovely suggestion."

They both knew there wasn't enough time left in their afternoon window to actually take advantage of it. Maybe if they hadn't bothered with lunch. Theo made a note to do the sex first next time. He liked hanging out with Wendy, but his desperation was becoming problematic.

She got a box for her remaining half sandwich and Theo gallantly took the pickle she didn't want. "I'm the pickle friend," Theo joked.

"Everyone needs a pickle friend," Wendy teased back. She glanced at his pants suggestively, and Theo almost choked on the pickle in his mouth.

They bundled back into their layers of coats and sweaters and ventured outside. It was either snowing lightly, or blowing off the trees. The wind was prickly and frigid.

"It's cruel to have the heat so high inside when it's this cold outside," Wendy complained, wrapping her scarf around her neck. "It gives me whiplash going back and forth."

"Are you suggesting that they keep the bakery at fridge temperatures inside so everyone has to eat their sandwiches wearing mittens?" Theo teased.

"I'm just saying that going from sweating in short sleeves to shivering in a down coat is some kind of torture," Wendy snorted. They had parked next to each other, and there was a tiny sliver of privacy from the buildings and bustling streets around them between the two vehicles.

"Wendy…" Theo could feel instinct swelling in him, even if he couldn't quite tell what it expected out of him. It wasn't like he could make love to her in the back of his frigid pickup, and they both had obligations. She needed to get back to work, and he had to pick Darius up in an hour. As much as he would have loved to spend that hour making sweet, dirty, desperate love to her, it wasn't terribly practical.

"If you're going to kiss me goodbye, you'd better do it before my lips freeze off," Wendy said crisply.

Theo didn't need a second invitation.

Her mouth was warm in the cool air, and their coats rustled and whispered as they crushed between them. The shape of her body beneath the down and nylon was tantalizing, and it was everything Theo could do not to grope her as they wrestled together in the parking lot with the very thin veneer of seclusion between their vehicles.

The cold went away altogether and Theo's world narrowed to the feel of her in his arms, the sound of the laughter he was kissing out of her, the taste of her in his mouth.

"Your sandwich had cilantro," Wendy said, when they broke apart.

Theo clapped a hand over his mouth. "Do I need a breath mint?"

"Lucky for you, I like cilantro."

"I like you."

The statement hung in the frozen air between them, along with the unspoken question. What *was* this?

"I…like you, too." Much like flustered-Wendy, suddenly-shy-Wendy was simply adorable.

"So, we're in like with each other?"

Wendy smiled. "This is a conversation more suited to Darius than to two grown-ups with mortgages and credit cards."

"Wendy," Theo said seriously. "I *really* like you…"

"Belle Lake Lookout *really*?" Wendy teased him.

Theo blinked at her without speaking, because what he really wanted to say was *forever really*. Could he ask this woman to be a mother to his children and a partner in his life? Did she *want* to be a mother? She knew his deepest secrets and certainly she was *into* him, but would he scare her off if he confessed how deep that ran?

"Definitely Belle Lake Lookout really," he agreed, trying to keep it light. "Maybe even cheap hotel really."

Wendy made a show of fanning herself. "Wow, what a charmer! I can't wait to make those bedsprings creak!"

Theo silently vowed to make bedsprings creak *soon* and gave her one last kiss, reluctant to peel himself out of her arms despite his frigid ears and the ticking clock.

"Miss me!" Wendy said merrily, finally pulling away and getting into her car. She had to get out and brush the snow off her windshield and back window. Theo helped her and then watched her drive away wistfully.

CHAPTER 24

"When you said you were seeing a single dad, you did not tell me you were dating a thirst trap from Las Vegas. How dare you hold that out on me!"

Wendy moved her yoga mat to the side to make room for her cousin. She and Addison both had punchcards to do drop-in classes and rarely attended if they didn't goad each other into it. This, with their busy schedules, meant that they usually met up in class once a month or so and moaned each time that it felt so good and they should do it more frequently…but then they never did.

"Isn't he a dreamboat?" Wendy agreed airily. "I think he must have been a stripper in Vegas, even though he hasn't admitted it. Can you imagine the tips he could make?"

Addison made a show of fanning herself. "I'd put dollar bills in that waistband!" She unrolled her mat and started stretching. "He also seems really *nice*."

"He's like if Mr. Rogers was sexy," Wendy said, then she wished she hadn't said it. "I'm such an unbelievable dork."

Addison, who had been balancing awkwardly to stretch her hamstrings, fell over on her side laughing. "No, I get it! He's like if wholesome had a baby with hot." She lowered her voice. "Have you tapped that yet?"

"What are we going to do, have hot sex in the DMV lobby while we wait for his license to print? He's got an eight-month-old baby and a surly twelve-year-old and both of them seem determined that my tenure as a nun continues as long as possible."

Addison sat up, reaching for her feet. Compared to Wendy, she was much more flexible. Wendy had always wondered if that was a trait related to being a shifter. "Does Daniel still hate you?"

"Darius," Wendy corrected. "And I don't think he hates me anymore, but he's also twelve and doesn't want us kissing in front of him and even though I think he's a pretty good kid, he's got school and theater and takes up plenty of Theo's time."

"Theo seems like a really good dad," Addison said admiringly. "He's probably worth waiting for."

"And waiting, and waiting," Wendy groused. "My lady bits are going to dry up and fall off before we get around to things."

"Stop, stop!" Addison said. "TMI!"

"You were the one who wanted to know if I'd tapped it yet," Wendy reminded her.

The other women in the room pretended not to listen and exchanged amused smiles as the instructor came bustling in to set up the stereo system and call the class to order.

Wendy had plenty of time to think about Theo as she went through the series of increasingly difficult poses. She had finally given him her cell number so that he didn't have to call her at the DMV, and they exchanged frequent texts. They weren't quite to the point of sexting, as people these days called it, but there was a definite *eggplant* edge to their conversations.

He wanted her, and she wanted him. It was just that he was a single dad and a relationship wasn't particularly convenient for either of them. When they did have a few minutes of privacy to snatch, it seemed much more important to use them for kissing than talking about a fuzzy unknown future. And there was never time or opportunity for anything *more*.

Was he as wound up as Wendy was? Her personal tools were getting more of a workout than they usually did, and she was still at a fever pitch of need she'd never known. Kissing was fun, but she was hungry for more.

Not just his body, but his company. Wendy caught herself at work wanting to make her inappropriate observations about her customers to him. She wanted to hear his tales about his work and his kids, even though she had never thought that children were interesting and had no fascination for food service. Theo had a droll way of storytelling that made her hang on his every word, and Wendy was amused to find it was only distantly related to her interest in other uses for his mouth.

She sighed. Drying out was not what her lady parts needed to be worried about right now, and she forced herself to stretch further and concentrate on the exercise.

"Oh my gosh," Addison said at the end of the class, as she always did. "I needed this so badly. Why don't we do this more often?"

"Those kids running you ragged?" Wendy chuckled. "We always say we're going to do this more regularly."

"This time I mean it!" Addison said, rolling up her mat. "And yes, it's wild at Cherry's right now. We got a new hire working full time, but we've still got a waitlist. Cherry's been looking for a bigger place!"

"Getting out from underneath Veronica Chase would be a nice bonus, too."

Addison frowned.

"Is she still poking around?"

"She's stopped trying to actively evict Cherry and is being really nice," Addison said, making sure that they weren't being overheard. The other women in the class were involved in their own chatter as they packed up their mats and blocks. "It's actually worse. I don't trust her."

"Find any more cameras?"

Addison shook her head. "Not since that one, and we do a sweep every morning now, inside and outside. But I swear, I feel like a tight rubber band at work. Those kids deserve a safe space, but what if it *isn't?*"

Addison didn't have to explain why it was so hard. Even though Wendy wasn't a shifter herself, a lot of the people she loved were, and she knew why the secret was so important.

All she had to do was watch the news to see how afraid people were of things that were strange and different. She wanted to believe that the public would embrace the wonder and joy of a world with an undercurrent of magic and enchantment, but she feared they would only see the secrets and be afraid and feel inferior and excluded.

Different was dangerous. And people who were afraid fell easily into the mob mentality. They would even turn on their neighbors and families, Wendy was sure.

The secret itself was a heavy burden, but letting the world know was a can of worms they didn't dare open.

Addison shook herself and gave a determined, sunny smile that Wendy recognized from the mirror. There was no point in dwelling on things they couldn't change. "We should have you and Theo over for Thanksgiving!" Addison said cheerfully. "Roderick wants to do a turkey, but we couldn't possibly eat it all ourselves. Gabby would love to have a baby who's littler than her to torture and take toys from."

"I don't know if Theo and I are at the Thanksgiving with the family stage yet," Wendy said cautiously. "I mean, he's hot, but we don't know each other *that* well."

"You won't know if you don't ask him," Addison pointed out. "Will you do it, or do I have to?"

"I don't need you to set me up with this guy," Wendy said impatiently.

"I'm not setting you up, I'm just giving you opportunities to get to know each other better," Addison said airily. "And at least your family isn't totally embarrassing like *mine*. I've got this cousin that I can't take in public."

Wendy gave a shout of laughter and bumped Addison with her hip. "Watch it. I still have the Halloween story in reserve."

Addison groaned. "I'll let you invite Theo to Thanksgiving yourself, and you have to promise not to tell it at the table."

"At the table?" Wendy said slyly.

"At all! Ever!"

"Fine, fine," Wendy agreed. "I'll invite him. But it's on you if the whole night is a disaster. Moody almost-teenager! Teleporting baby! *Me!* It will inevitably be chaos!"

CHAPTER 25

Theo wasn't sure how he managed to forget how much work it was getting two kids out of the house when he did it so regularly. He never seemed to calculate enough time to get them ready. Darius dragged around cradling his wrist like an invalid when he remembered to, and Jackson required two diaper changes.

"I'm so sorry we're late," he said as Wendy opened the door to Roderick and Addison's house.

"Are you *really* sorry?" she teased him. "I could find a glass of water."

How was it that they had inside jokes already? She wore a plain white apron over a skirt covered in turkeys, and there was a smudge of flour on one cheek. Her hair was clipped back in sequined barrettes over her ears and Theo marveled at how dear she could be after just a few weeks of barely knowing each other. He might have kissed her smiling lips, but Darius gave a groan of disgust at his elbow and Theo didn't want to embarrass him.

"You're not too late," Wendy said, stepping aside to let

them in. "Roderick is just getting the turkey out of the oven and it has to rest for a few minutes."

Roderick's house was small for all the people in it. There were two tables pressed together and filling up the living room, draped in mis-matched tablecloths. One was Christmas green and red, the other ivory, and they were surrounded by an assortment of chairs. There were two high chairs, and one of them was emblazoned with the Tiny Paws logo—Addison must have borrowed it for the event. A puppy was romping on the floor, and Theo was surprised that Jackson stayed in human form long enough to be wrestled out of his snowsuit. He seemed satisfied with keeping his fingers and toes and crawled after the wolf puppy, shrieking in joy.

Roderick proved to be a broad-shouldered Black man with an easy smile and a ruffled pink apron, and he left the kitchen long enough to greet the newcomers and shake their hands before disappearing again.

Dana was a petite Black woman that Wendy introduced. "This is Dana. She's Gabby's birth mom."

"Nice to meet you," Dana said, shaking Theo's hand. She seemed serene about being Roderick's ex, and Theo knew better than to inquire about the dynamics of a relationship that invited her to holiday dinners.

Theo expected Darius to retreat to the couch and sulk until food was served, and was surprised when the boy took off his coat and sat straight down with Jackson and Gabby to play with them. He was careful to draw the two kids out from underfoot, gently redirecting them with toys as Wendy, Addison, and Dana brought food out of the kitchen to spread on the tables.

"Can I help?" Theo asked.

"I think staying out of the way is as much a help as anything," Wendy said, pointing him to a seat at the table.

"You want something to drink? There's white wine open, and sparkling cider. Roderick's got beers in the fridge."

"A glass of wine sounds great," Theo said, sitting where he was directed. There was a television with football on in the living room, and although the sound was down, it was far from quiet in the house. A kitchen timer was going off, Gabby was barking, and Jackson had already found the noisiest toy in the bin.

"Dinner!" Addison called, carrying in a huge turkey on a groaning platter of roasted potatoes and carrots. "I told you we had too much to eat by ourselves!"

Roderick, still wearing his pink apron, carved the turkey while Darius—completely oblivious to the wrist brace that had been an excuse for everything just an hour ago—swept a protesting Jackson up and buckled him into the highchair. Addison coaxed Gabby back into human form by promising blueberries and dressed her with the efficiency of a lot of practice.

Wendy sat comfortably next to Theo and Darius sat opposite him, with Jackson between them at the end of the table.

"Let's have a moment of gratitude," Roderick said from the head of the table. He led them in a swift, heartfelt grace punctuated in intervals by Jackson's outrage at being in a highchair, and then said merrily, "Now dig in!"

"Don't let it get cold!" Addison urged.

Between the babies, the spread of food, and the muted football game, there was plenty of easy conversation. Addison and Dana appeared to be fast friends. Roderick was quiet but friendly, and proud of the dinner he'd provided. Theo had tried to bring something but had been told by Wendy that Roderick was from the south and would be offended if he couldn't provide for his guests.

"This is a great turkey," Theo said, without stretching

for the compliment. He kicked Darius under the table to remind him to be grateful.

Darius stopped shoveling food in his mouth long enough to say, "Delicious, thanks!"

Jackson tried everything, from cubes of turkey meat to a messy handful of green bean casserole. He devoured most of a biscuit without pausing for breath and made memorable faces over the cranberry dressing before pushing the rest off his tray. Gabby was to the point of using a spoon, but she mostly used it to smash her potatoes and play percussion over the conversation.

Addison was clearly a fan of the losing football team, and Roderick needled her affectionately as the meal progressed. "There's still time!" she protested, craning to view a replay. "They could come back!"

"Twenty points in a quarter?"

"More impossible things have happened!"

Theo wondered if he imagined Addison's amused glance at Wendy, and what it meant.

Wendy herself was no less outrageous than ever, and more than once, laughter stalled eating.

Theo helped himself to seconds of everything, and Darius took thirds. The dishes on the table dwindled, but only the olives disappeared completely. Jackson ate eleven of them and Theo was afraid to feed him any more.

There was a lull at the end of the meal, everyone adjusting their waistbands and groaning in pleasure.

"I haven't eaten so well since I got stuck with an extra surf and turf after being abandoned for dinner," Wendy said, poking Theo in the side.

Apparently, she'd told Addison and Dana some version of that story, because they both smirked knowingly.

"There's pie!" Addison said cheerfully. "Pumpkin, pecan, and apple."

"You didn't have to make three pies," Dana protested.

"I wouldn't be a good host if there weren't options," Addison said.

"I'm not going to be a good guest if I explode," Dana countered.

"I'm uncomfortably stuffed," Wendy said. "Can we have a break first?" She leaned towards Theo. "Addison's pecan pie is not to be missed if you can help it."

Addison looked pleased. "Maybe we should clear the dishes and wait a little while to make room!"

"Let me help clean up," Theo said swiftly. "You guys have been so generous."

Roderick kissed Addison on the head as he stood. "Let the menfolk clean up the kitchen," he said. "You can watch your team lose horribly and make room for pie."

Theo expertly gathered half the plates off the table into his arms as he got to his feet.

"I'm impressed!" Dana said.

Addison whistled in awe.

"He's good at lots of stuff," Wendy said proudly, setting off a flurry of giggles. "Not that, you filthy people. I wouldn't know about that. Get your brains out of the gutter!"

Darius looked like he wanted to sink into his chair and die, and Theo figured that was some kind of holiday meal milestone.

"I think Jackson needs to be changed," Darius said desperately.

"There's a changing table in Gabby's room," Dana said, pushing back her chair. "I'll show you where."

Theo followed Roderick into the kitchen and set to washing the many dishes that wouldn't fit in the dishwasher.

"Thanks again for having us over," Theo said gratefully.

"Really happy to," Roderick said. "Holidays should be shared."

Their conversation was carefully neutral at first, limited to praise for the meal, talk about the weather, but it swiftly eased into discussion about their kids, swapping stories about the hair-raising stress of raising shifter children.

"It's been a learning experience," Theo said, adding another squirt of soap to the sink. "Who knew that shopping would be such a gauntlet? All these complications I never expected!"

"Didn't you already go through this with Darius?" Roderick asked, taking a cookie sheet to dry and put away.

Theo gave him a sideways look. It was ironic that Darius *not* being a shifter was his secret, and he decided it wouldn't hurt if Roderick knew. Addison's boyfriend knew about Wendy, and Addison knew about Darius, so it was really only a matter of time. It might keep him from saying something uncomfortable in front of the boy.

"Darius isn't actually a shifter."

Roderick stopped his towel mid-swipe. "He's not?"

"I know he feels like one. It's a bit like Wendy, I guess, just an anomaly."

Roderick resumed drying. "Fair enough. So this is all new, then?"

"I've had Jackson for…" Theo had to do some quick math. Halloween to Thanksgiving. "Almost four weeks now."

"And his mom…?"

How did Theo explain Juliette? *He* didn't even understand Juliette. "She's not a shifter, either." He didn't volunteer any more details about her. "She—*we*—decided Jackson would be better off with someone who was."

"How does Darius like that?"

Theo took a moment to consider his response, and Roderick took his quiet for reluctance. "Sorry, man, that's pretty personal."

"No, it's fine," Theo said quickly. "He's been a trooper. He adores Jackson and I don't know what I would have done without him. But I know it's got to be tough on him. He was an only kid, and now he's got a baby brother eating all my time and sleep. And not just a baby brother, but a shifter baby brother who can—" Theo stopped himself before he brought up teleporting. Some secrets still needed to be kept. "Do everything he can't," he ended haltingly.

"He seems like a good kid," Roderick said kindly, not prying if he noticed Theo's hesitation. "Real polite. He certainly enjoyed the food."

Theo laughed. "He's at a bottomless stage. He'd come back in here and eat that much again if I let him."

There was a shriek from the living room as someone on the television did something terrible or wonderful—Theo couldn't tell.

That took their conversation to the topic of sports. Theo was more of a hockey fan than football, and Roderick admitted a love for baseball.

"The most boring sport to watch next to bowling," Roderick said sheepishly.

"Or poker."

"Is poker a sport?"

"According to broadcast television," Theo laughed. He marveled that he had come to Thanksgiving dinner fearing the worst, and he might have come away with a new friend.

CHAPTER 26

*W*endy left her pile of dishes—half the size of
Theo's professional armload and much less
gracefully managed—in the kitchen. "Don't let me inter-
rupt this lovely moment of masculine domesticity," she
said, giving Theo's butt a smart snap with a towel. "That's
the last of the dishes."

She thought that Theo might have kissed her if
Roderick hadn't been there, studiously drying a skillet and
pretending not to exist.

"I'm going to go see if Addison's team has lost yet," she
said, acting like she hadn't been hoping for that kiss.

Addison's team had actually closed the gap considerably, and the game was in its final ten minutes, which
Wendy knew from experience meant maybe an hour of
television. Dana and Addison were both sitting on the
literal edges of their seats, riveted to a few zebra-dressed
officials arguing over blades of grass.

"I'll just...go see how Darius is doing with the kids,"
Wendy offered. She regretted not bringing any knitting
with her. She'd been sure that it would be date-killing to

have crafting on hand and told herself that she should make conversation and try to be normal. As if Thanksgiving with an odd patchwork extended family really counted as a date anyway. As if she could ever be normal.

She paused in Gabby's door to find Darius sitting on the floor with the younger kids. Gabby was showing him all of her toys and snatching them away with her dark curls flouncing. "Mine!" she said shrilly, if he tried to take one that she offered. "Mine!" She paid no attention to Jackson, who was standing uncertainly at the bottom of the changing table, looking up at it like he might try to scale it if his knees weren't made of rubber. He was bouncing a little in place and Wendy expected him to fall over at any moment.

Darius looked up and saw her. Wendy tried to decipher his expression and failed. She didn't think it was entirely hostile.

"Your dad is having man chat with Roderick in the kitchen and Addison and Dana are bonding over football. Mind if I hang with you and the rugrats?"

Darius shrugged. "Whatever." He pulled his feet in closer when Wendy sat across the floor from him, so they wouldn't accidentally touch. Her skirt fanned out over her knees, and Wendy wondered in chagrin if turkeys had been too juvenile to wear.

"Mine!" Gabby said firmly, waving a stuffed blueberry at Wendy. "Mine."

Jackson finally succumbed to gravity and sank down to hands and knees so he could crawl to Wendy with a flattering cry of happy greeting. Outside the room, Addison and Dana gave shouts of protest and dismay over a ruling that had finally been made.

Wendy's keys fell out of her pocket as Jackson scrabbled at her side, and he promptly picked them up and put the key fob in his mouth.

"Don't let him chew on that," Darius warned. "The batteries in there are really dangerous."

Wendy went to take her keys back, but Jackson had strong fingers and she didn't want to hurt him.

"Distract him with a toy," Darius suggested. He tossed her one with his braced hand—it clearly wasn't bothering him anymore.

Jackson didn't particularly care about the safari animal teething ring, but he was diverted just long enough for Wendy to pull her keys away.

Wendy put her slobbery key fob back in her skirt pocket. Jackson shrieked and tried to get in after it, dropping the disdained teething ring. She swung him up into her lap instead, and he was completely uncooperative, first squirming with more strength than a loaf of bread ought to have, then going unexpectedly boneless. He got loose, and Wendy let him ooze down her legs back to the floor without trying to restrain him further.

Gabby laughed and clapped her hands, then bolted for the door.

"Gabby!" Darius called without getting up. "I've got your blueberry! Yum, I'm going to eat it!"

Gabby paused in the doorway, deliberating, then gave a yip that was part laugh and part scream before racing unsteadily back to fall into Darius and grab for her stuffy.

"You're good with babies," Wendy said grudgingly. "Really patient."

"They're just like animals," Darius said solemnly. "You can't get mad at them for being what they are."

Wendy hesitated. "Speaking of animals…"

"Are we going to do some of that gross heart-to-heart stuff?"

Wendy gave a surprised laugh. "No, I mean, we don't have to. I was just curious if your friends at school knew you weren't a shifter."

Darius gave her what could only be called stink-eye. "Did my dad tell you my friends were shifters?" He bopped Gabby gently in the face with the plush blueberry and she giggled and fell back on her butt, looking not at all put out.

"Mine!"

"Theo? No. I saw them at Career Day. I know you kids think you are super slick, but you're really not."

Darius's look went from sour to surprised. "You could...tell?"

"Not with magic or anything," Wendy was quick to assure him. "I'm not a shifter, so I don't have instinct. But I'm not blind or stupid, and shifters all have this *I'm being sooooo careful* air about them, and a bit of this aura of ego, you know?"

Darius surprised Gabby by letting her pull the blueberry away from him. After a moment of confusion, the little girl tried to give it back to him. "Mine!"

Darius was looking thoughtfully at Wendy, clearly trying to decide what to say, and she gave him space, poking Jackson to see if he would do anything else entertaining. The baby seemed to have forgotten about her key fob and was rolling around on the carpet rather aimlessly. Wendy kept having moments of worry—would he roll into something sharp? Was he going to get dizzy and throw up? But he bounced harmlessly off of everything he hit, and didn't seem to mind which direction was up or down.

"My mom can sense shifters," Darius said slowly. "Even though she isn't one."

Wendy told herself to act normal, not to overreact to news that Darius clearly felt was special.

Normal wasn't really her strong point, though. "That's

so cool! I've never heard of that before. Are there shifters in her family? All of my family are lynx shifters. I always thought I would be, too...and never was." Wendy made herself shut her mouth. She had a terrible habit of trying to make herself sound like she was relating and instead making it sound like it was all about her.

"Mom didn't really talk about her family," Darius said, and Wendy worried that she'd accidentally offended him. Sometimes, she feared that was what she did best.

"It's not so bad," she said earnestly. "I mean, not being a shifter. I mean, you aren't less of a person for not being one. If anything, you're more of a person. A human person. Sorry, I'm really terrible at this crap." Was crap a bad word? "*Stuff.*"

"Did you ever think that there's something wrong with your head?" Darius asked wistfully. "Like you aren't wired right to be a shifter? Like there isn't space for an animal in there? I mean, you're really...uh…"

"Weird?" Wendy supplied.

Darius was playing another lazy game of tug-a-war with Gabby and her blueberry plush, trying not to meet Wendy's eyes. "*Different,*" he said firmly.

Wendy watched Darius. He didn't look a lot like his dad, but some of the lines of Theo's face were there. "Do you mean like ADHD or ADD or whatever it's called? Do you feel like that describes you?"

Darius shot her an anxious look and gave a shrug with one shoulder. He had switched hands with Gabby and was cradling his braced wrist in his lap.

Wendy recognized the fragile moment and paused to consider her words. "They weren't really big on diagnosing those things when I was in school. People with different brains had to fend for themselves and develop their own coping methods, and depending on how successful they

—*we*—were, got defined as either *gifted* or *difficult*. Sometimes both. It's changed a lot since then, though. If your brain is getting in your own way, it can help to have someone poke at it. There have been a lot of medical advancements, and I know there's drugs some people swear by."

Darius didn't give her any help by keeping up his end of the conversation and Wendy plowed on. "Theo says you're doing well in school, but you strike me as the type who could be flailing and covering it up really well because you're smart, and you should tell your dad if you're struggling."

Jackson had rolled back to Wendy's side and apparently remembered that there was something interesting in her pocket. Wendy pulled him up into her lap with more success this time. "Oh, you are *gross*, kid. How are you so droolly?"

"Here." Darius tossed her a thin little blanket printed with monkeys and Wendy guessed she was meant to mop the baby up with it. Jackson thought this was a great game and giggled and grabbed at it while Wendy wiped his face, once again forgetting about the treasure in her pocket.

She was still thinking about Darius's theory. "I don't know if being neurodivergent or whatever makes it harder to be a shifter. I've met some really strange shifters who were probably on the spectrum, but you don't really talk about that, right? Well, most people don't. People with boundaries and internal editors."

Jackson chose that moment to shift, flowing into an upside-down griffin with downy flightless wings spread out on Wendy's lap. The sleeper he was wearing split at the seams and the diaper ripped with the sound of Velcro. Jackson snapped his beak at the towel and got one of Wendy's fingers.

"Ow! Don't bite me, you little shi—er, um…"

Darius guffawed.

"*Shifter*. I was going to say shifter," Wendy fibbed.

Darius laughed harder.

Jackson released her finger and the towel and gave a remorseful little chirp, wriggling the rest of his clothing off.

"Sorry," Wendy said in chagrin, ruffling the downy feathers on Jackson's belly. It was hard to tell where soft feathers transformed to fluffy fur. "I'm not really mom material."

"Lots of moms swear," Darius told her kindly.

Gabby, realizing that none of the attention was on her anymore, shifted into her puppy form and shrugged out of her own torn clothing to attack the dark tip of Jackson's tail.

"You know, it would be a lot easier if someone designed a range of kids clothing for shifters," Wendy said thoughtfully, reaching for the parts of Jackson's romper that were spread on her skirt as he rolled off and went to clumsily protect his tail. "Put easy-release snaps or laces all down the sides and you can just close them back up and save a lot of ruined clothing in the long run."

"Like a line of rompers for shifters?" Darius said, gathering up Gabby's. "What do most shifters with kids do?" Wendy remembered Jackson was very new in his life, and he hadn't grown up with a lot of shifters like she had.

"Let them run around naked until they reach a certain age?" Wendy said. "It works when you're growing up in a private home or a really tight community, but less well in public."

"Bet you could make a lot of money in Nickel City making clothes for baby shifters," Darius said. "There are a lot of shifters here."

"The last thing I need is another project," Wendy said,

but she was still looking at Jackson's clothes. The seam was actually the strongest point, so the fabric had failed around it, which would be really hard to repair more than once or twice. She could see that someone already had.

"Don't bite, Jackson," Darius said, poking the gryphon lightly in the side when he got rough with the larger puppy. "Gentle beak!" Jackson didn't pay the slightest attention to him, but Gabby didn't seem to mind, and they were wrestling whole-heartedly, growling and rolling around on the carpet.

"Your dad isn't going to pick me over you, you know," Wendy blurted.

Darius was surprised enough to look up at her. His eyes were just like Theo's, all golden-warm and unguarded.

"I mean, if you made him choose. And I wouldn't ask him to. In case you were worried."

"I wasn't worried," Darius mumbled.

Outside the bedroom, there was a chorus of protests and outrage as the final moments of the football game went the direction that none of them wanted it to. It sounded as if Theo and Roderick had joined Dana and Addison. Was Theo a football person? Did it matter? There was so much that Wendy didn't know about him.

"Sounds like it's time for pie," she said, rising to her feet. "You want some help getting these twerps dressed again? I can probably figure out which limbs go where if you can get them back into less furry forms."

Gabby was able to help herself a little once Darius had coaxed them back to human with promises of pie, but Jackson had no interest in wearing one of her smaller sleepers and fought Wendy for every appendage.

"Gotcha!" she said, when the last button was closed and he was muttering in defeat.

She looked up to find Theo at the door, watching them with a sappy smile on his face.

Jackson gave a cry of greeting and rolled to hands and knees to crawl over and pull himself up on Theo's leg.

Wendy resisted her desire to do the same and got to her own feet. "Pie?" she said hopefully.

"I'm hungry," Darius said, even though she'd just watched him tuck a few pounds of Thanksgiving dinner away. He bounced up, pushing off on his braced wrist like he'd forgotten it again.

Wendy followed him thoughtfully. She'd been honest when she tried to assure Darius that he wasn't less of a person for not being a shifter. And if that was true for him, why shouldn't she believe it for herself?

CHAPTER 27

Theo stared at his phone, desperate for a reply, as tightly wound as a twisted playground swing with a child in the seat, ready to spin until they were sick.

His own message was on the screen, showing as read: *Darius has offered (!!) to babysit so I can take you out to dinner. Are you available?*

Was it too abrupt? Should he send a heart or an emoji or something? Should he have specified that he meant tonight, or was it clear enough?

He was just telling himself it was stupid to keep staring at the phone, that he should put it down and do something else, watched pots and all, when her response flashed up with a cheerful burble.

Sure! I can be ready in fifteen minutes.

Theo grinned stupidly at his phone for a good three of those minutes, and then went to run fingers through his hair and shave. He still needed a haircut, but there never seemed to be time.

Jackson was stacking blocks with Darius. A colorful

kid's cartoon was playing on the television. "We'll be fine, Dad. I'll text if he teleports and I'll tire him out for bed."

"You're the best. I'll be home by nine," Theo promised. "Eight-thirty?"

"Ten is fine, Dad. I'm almost thirteen."

"Nine-thirty."

"Stop being weird."

"That's a tall order."

Theo kissed them both on their heads, to Jackson's bird-like squawk of delight and Darius's exclamation of disgust.

Theo had to remind himself that having a legal Montana driver's license was no excuse to speed to Wendy's house through slushy snow.

"Did you have a place in mind?" Wendy asked as she opened the door, wearing her coat over a long, swishy skirt.

Theo didn't pause to admire her, but picked up exactly where they'd left off on his porch the week before, swooping to catch Wendy in his arms and kiss her desperately.

"I'm good with DoorDash," she said between kisses, and she kicked the door closed behind him and wrestled his coat off his shoulders as he kicked off his boots.

They stripped each other swiftly, nibbling at exposed skin as they went, and Wendy drew him back down the hallway. Focused entirely on her, Theo ran them into a closed door and tried to open it and draw her into it. Wendy giggled against his mouth.

"That's the bathroom! Try the next door," she suggested.

The next door opened into a bedroom unlike any other room in the very eclectic house. It was hung with tapestries on the ceiling and every wall, and lined in tidy bookshelves. Cloth-covered lamps gave a muted light and everything here was atmosphere. It made Theo realize that the rest of her house was very well lit, all but flooded with bright work lights. This was intimate, and her bed was a giant altar to comfort, with fluffy throws and pillows of all textures and sparkle.

It smelled faintly of pine sap and patchouli, and the floor was plush under Theo's stockinged feet.

She could not possibly have done all this in the fifteen minutes she'd had to prepare. Theo doubted that she could have done this even if she'd worked all night on it. No, this was the bedroom of a woman who was determined to have a decadent personal space, exactly to her own taste, and Theo loved it and was honored to be invited in.

Wendy was trying to get his pants off. "These need an escape cord," she said, probably not accidentally groping him with one hand as she fumbled with his button with the other. "Where's a pair of rip-off pants when you need them?"

"About that…"

Wendy paused with her hand still caressing his cock through the fabric. "Yes?"

"You were right. Sort of."

"You *were* a stripper," Wendy said in triumph.

"I was an escort. I did shows or parties sometimes, but mostly I was a personal hire."

Wendy didn't let go of him, but her fingers stilled. It made it very difficult to think, but Theo plowed on. "I don't want to have any weird surprises or dealbreakers later."

"Because you're not at all about weird surprises," Wendy reminded him.

"That is kind of my theme," Theo admitted.

"Did you sleep with them?" Wendy asked directly. She

still hadn't moved her hand from his penis, and Theo recognized that this was a very fraught moment.

"Not for money," Theo said emphatically. "I never drank on the job, and I never let a client do something they might regret. I was there to be arm candy, to protect them, and to show them a good time out on the town. If they called me the next day to hook up, it was never part of our contract."

Wendy did remove her hand then. "Did that happen often?" she asked dangerously.

"A lot less than you'd think," Theo said honestly. "Is it a problem?"

To his relief, she laughed. "Honestly, no. I'm not going to get all snobby about sex work, if that's what you're worried about. My life has been a lot more chaste than I'd prefer, but I won't judge anyone for having a past or a fun time or what sounds like a really great job."

"I'd rather you didn't, you know, tell a lot of people. Darius has enough trouble fitting in without his dad being a joy boy from Vegas." As soon as he'd said it, Theo wished he hadn't.

"A *joy boy*? Is that what they call it these days?" Wendy had to cling to him for balance, she was laughing so hard now. "No, it's okay, your secret is safe with me. I promise not to call you that, *ever*."

"I appreciate that," Theo said gravely.

"But if I offer you money, will you take off your clothes and dance for me?"

"If you pay me, I can't have sex with you," Theo reminded her.

"So, it's one or the other," Wendy drawled. "Either I get to sleep with you or I have to pay for the pleasure of your company. That's a tough choice, Mr. Royal."

Theo pretended to search his pockets. "I think I have a copy of my standard contract in here," he said.

"Paperwork? Are there forms to fill out? You know how to get into *my* pants, pretty boy."

"I can work with *pretty boy*," Theo said, grinning. "Want me to show you how to get mine off?"

His erection hadn't gone anywhere during his confession, which hadn't made speaking or thinking much easier, and Wendy's hiss of appreciation made it even harder.

CHAPTER 28

$\mathscr{W}$endy had worried that she'd lived like a nun too long and she wouldn't know what to do with a real live man in her bed once she actually got him there, but between her own body's undeniable responses and Theo's skilled fingers, everything was absolutely *perfect*.

Every time she ran into some insurmountable problem —like how did she get out of her own shirt? and how was *that* going to fit where she desperately wanted it?—Theo was there, patiently unbuttoning her blouse and uncovering her hungry breasts, then baring his own body bit by delicious bit. Wendy forgot to wonder if she remembered how slot A and tab B worked and could only admire him for a moment.

His parts stood at certain attention, and after only a moment, Wendy dared to touch him, trailing her fingers down his chest and taking his cock in her hand. She stroked the length of it and reveled in the power she clearly had over him as he shuddered in her fingers.

Wendy could have spent much longer playing with his penis, pulling on his balls, seeing how much pressure made

Theo hiss in pain and pleasure, watching him rise to a fever pitch, but he finally stopped her. "I have a condom."

Wendy blinked. She hadn't even thought about that. "The ones in my bedside table are probably expired," she realized wryly. "At least one of us still has some mental capacity left, because I sure don't."

Theo kissed her again and Wendy was glad that he didn't seem to be any more tired of that than she was. Her lips were burning, but no more than the rest of her was at this point.

He had to stoop to find his pants pocket and the promised condom, and Wendy sat down on the edge of her bed and watched him in absolute appreciation. He was so gorgeous. The lines of his body, the length of his legs, the muscles in his core, his arms, his shoulders…Wendy couldn't find a favorite place to settle her gaze.

Then he was smoothing the condom on over his cock, and she knew exactly where to watch.

He made it a show, posing with one arm up and his hip thrust out, and Wendy smirked to think that she'd been at least a little bit right about his secret stripping career. It didn't change anything. If anything, it felt like a moment from a fantasy that he was bringing straight to life.

Then, without more showmanship, he was straddling her, tipping her back on the bed, and pressing her open. She was dripping wet by then, and he slid in with the barest, most delicious, resistance.

She might have been right to worry about his size, but it didn't matter when he was there, filling her so perfectly, and moving just right inside of her. Every delve he made was just deep enough and desperately not quite enough. Wendy couldn't make sense of her own sensations, like she was two people inside of herself, both of them totally focused on being exactly where and what she was supposed to be, with this amazing man who was showing her places of pleasure she'd never known.

"Don't come yet," Theo warned her, slowing his strokes and drawing out.

"Why *not?*" Wendy wanted to know, all but clawing at his shoulders. Her whole body was on fire now, not just her aching pussy, but all the way to her toes and her ears. Everything about her wanted everything about him.

"Because if I hear you come now, I'm not going to be able to stop myself," Theo said between clenched teeth. His breath was ragged and Wendy could feel the pulse of him everywhere they touched.

Wendy gave a cry of loss as he lifted himself off of her and kissed down her neck. She was utterly helpless to his touch, whimpering and arching desperately after him.

"Shh, shh," he said, kissing down to her breasts. He paused and suckled at one nipple, making Wendy writhe and beg as he toyed with the opposite breast using his fingers.

"Theo, please…" She couldn't exist on this edge of excitement; it wasn't possible to be here so long.

Then he moved further down, one hand teasing her clit as the other cupped the cheek of her ass.

"Are you…?"

Then his mouth landed where his cock had been.

It wasn't anything like being filled by his thick, hard member, but it was just as amazing to have his tongue there, and twice as tantalizing. He played her clit with his fingers and sucked and teased her with his tongue and Wendy couldn't keep herself from the cliff of passion and didn't try.

She didn't recognize that she cried out until the moment was done and her throat was dry and her body was coursing with pleasure and release.

Theo lingered there, gently easing her back to awareness with kisses and caresses, until he finally gave a growl of his own need and then he was turning her over on the bed. He held her down firmly with one hand on her arm, spread her lips, and surged into her again.

Their lovemaking before had been gentle and careful, and this was everything Wendy had wanted to beg for: desperate, primal rutting. He plunged into her, again and again, holding her with both hands now, his breath hot on her neck as he coupled close, stroke after sizzling stroke.

Wendy came again, hot and hard, her cries muffled in the pillows that she clutched as Theo drove her deeper and harder into them.

There was a smaller third crest as he slowed and his motions went frantic and jerky with his own release. He groaned and Wendy felt all his muscles go tense, then he was choking, "Yes, yes…!" and going limp at last.

They fell apart from each other and Wendy gasped for air as she rolled out of the pillows. Her body was still thrumming and the aftershocks of her orgasms echoed through all her limbs.

After a few moments, Theo took off his condom and tied it off, dropping it in the trash can by the bed. He cleaned off with a few tissues and Wendy followed suit, too dazed and delirious still to dread the awkward after moments or wonder what came next.

Theo came back to the bed just as she began to feel chilled and think about getting dressed, and wrapped his arms around her and tucked her close as a small spoon. He warmed her and completed her and comforted her and Wendy couldn't understand how this was somehow better than the world-rocking release he'd just given her.

After a moment, she remembered *joy boy* and broke into hysterical giggles.

Theo laughed with her, and they were both so full of happiness and endorphins that it didn't really matter what either of them was finding mirth in.

"Thank you," she said, when her laughter had subsided enough.

"Thank *you*," Theo replied, kissing her ear.

"I should send you a thank-you card," Wendy decided.

"I should send you a fruit basket," Theo said.

"Oh, is this how it's going to be?" Wendy teased. "Always trying to one-up each other?"

"I'll send you a thank you *goat*," Theo suggested. "Top that."

"Don't challenge me, Mr. Royal."

Theo's arms tightened on her and his whole body tensed. Wendy wondered what she'd said wrong. Was it a stage name after all?

Before she could decide what to say to make him relax again, there was a buzz from the doorway where they'd left their clothing. "Is that your phone?"

Theo got up to check it.

Wendy watched him stoop to find his phone, openly appreciating his lanky bare body and graceful gait, and she was just wondering how much longer she could convince him to stay when she felt a little zing of alarm and warning from no particular source. All of his muscles seemed to tense.

"What is it?" she asked, sitting up. "Did Darius lose Jackson?"

Theo turned back to her, confusion and worry all over his gorgeous face. "Juliette is coming into town. She says she can finally tell me everything."

CHAPTER 29

Theo played with the coffee that he didn't want to drink. He certainly wasn't going to order something stronger to meet with Juliette.

But he wasn't thinking about Juliette as he waited, checking his watch and his phone for any updates.

Mr. Royal.

Wendy had called him Mr. Royal, and Theo had opened his mouth to call her Mrs. Royal in return.

It had been incredible sex, absolutely mind-blowing and life-altering, and he'd wanted to propose to her on the spot, which was absolutely insane and he couldn't figure out why his gryphon was leaning on him to do it.

I'm not asking her to marry me while we're still sticky from sex and high on dopamine or whatever, he told his gryphon smartly. *That's the dumbest thing in the world.*

She'd say yes, his gryphon said confidently. *She's where we are meant to be.*

His animal had always been more attuned to instinct than he was, better able to sense its currents and interpret its messages. But that didn't mean that Theo was going to blunder along doing what a feather-headed mythical free-loader in his head told him to do.

When we ask her to marry us, it will be with Darius's blessing, and a ring, and the right words. Not giggling together like teenagers in the back of a station wagon.

His gryphon, always literal-minded, couldn't understand what a station wagon had to do with anything.

Then Juliette walked into the bar, and Theo was relieved to discover that any lingering feelings he'd feared he'd harbored for the mother of his children were gone.

"Neutral ground, I guess?" Juliette said, looking around at the seedy dive. She slipped onto the bench across from him and flagged down the waitress. "I'll have a rum and coke."

"I couldn't think of another place that would be open this late, but not crowded, where we could speak privately. Was Jackson in danger in Las Vegas? Is he still? What do you have to tell me? Why can you, suddenly?"

"I made the agency give me authorization," Juliette said. "You deserve to know the truth. *All* of the truth."

That was the last answer Theo was expecting. "I think you'd better start at the beginning."

"I work for a Federally authorized shifter protection and espionage organization in Vegas, and they started to notice that shifters were going missing a few months ago. I went undercover investigating a scientific organization—a gene company—that seemed a little too interested in rumors of shapeshifters. We think they're trying to back-wards engineer a shifter serum. I got too close to their secrets, and I knew that they would love to get their hands on a gryphon shifting baby. As soon as I realized that Jackson was going to be shifting, I knew he was at risk with me."

With every word, Theo got more and more uncomfortable. A scientific company that was *capturing shifters?* Juliette was a *spy?* A secret agent? He'd thought—*hoped*—that Juliette's worries were nothing more than the usual attempt to keep shifters secret. But now it sounded more like an active danger. "So, when you used to tell me you worked for an *agency*, it apparently wasn't an *acting* agency, or an *escort* agency."

"I never said that it was," Juliette reminded him.

She's telling the truth, his gryphon assured him, as full of worry as Theo himself was. *But not all the truth.*

That was their entire relationship in a nutshell, Theo thought. But he certainly wasn't volunteering that he and Jackson could *teleport*, so maybe he was just as much to blame.

Juliette paused at the approach of the waitress and gave her a bright, fake smile. "Thanks, hon!"

She took a bracing sip before going on. "That's why I brought you Jackson. They've got at least one shifter working for them who would know *he* was a shifter. If they brought their sniffer around Jackson, they'd know what he was. I knew you could protect him, like I couldn't."

"And now something's changed?" Theo guessed. "You didn't come here *just* to tell me no one is in any danger."

Juliette smiled ruefully. "I don't know for sure, but gossipy neighbors probably noticed that I suddenly packed up my eight-month-old son and sent him away. Suspicious bosses might have put two and two together and come up with four. I'm suddenly locked out of a lot of the systems I once had access to, so I know that they don't trust me anymore, but I don't know how far that goes. My name is probably on a list. The agency made the call to relocate me for my own safety and gave me the green light to come see the kids and tell you about my work before I went."

"How much peril are we talking about?" Theo wanted to know. "How likely is it they might follow you here?"

"Not likely," Juliette said confidently. "I'm good at dodging tails and you very conveniently moved a really long drive away. I've kept my absences short, only pay cash when I travel, and my phone is on a private server. I doubt they know where I am."

"This is what you've been keeping from me all this time."

Juliette was silent for a moment. "It wasn't like I wanted to. The agency's rules are really strict."

"We had kids together, Juliette. Why now?"

She was quiet again, and Theo had to sort through his feelings of betrayal and anger...and relief. He'd been able to think of so many worse things that her distance might have meant. This made a certain amount of sense.

"I *made* them let me," Juliette finally said. "I realized how unfair it was, and how much it bothered me. I played the card that I couldn't do my work as well, knowing that you were in the dark and wouldn't know what danger signs to watch out for."

Theo chewed on that, and their conversation halted as the waitress checked in to see if they wanted more drinks. Juliette smiled and conversed with the waitress easily. Theo had always known she was a talented actress, but he'd never witnessed her sliding between parts so seamlessly.

"Where are you relocating?" Theo asked, when the waitress left.

Juliette took a sip of her drink. "A place in Alaska. Shkalnik. Don't think I didn't want to come here. I miss Jackson. I miss Darius, even though I know he's still mad at me for not being the mom he wanted me to be."

"So mad," Theo agreed. "But he sometimes gets mad about the wrong socks, too."

"How are they doing?" Juliette asked wistfully. "Both of the kids. Are they…well?"

Theo opened his mouth to tell her about the day care for shifters where Jackson was thriving and snapped it shut again. Even if she meant well and worked for a well-meaning agency, that information was dangerous to share. If these people might go after a gryphon infant, what would they make of a Chinese unicorn or an elemental? What lengths would they go to capture more special children? He hated that he couldn't be blindly trusting and thought he understood a little of what Juliette had suffered keeping her secrets.

"Darius is in the school show of A Christmas Carol," he said, as mildly as he could. "He's Bob Cratchit. We've been drilling lines a lot."

There was longing in Juliette's eyes. "I wish I could see him on stage," she said. "I wish we could do Christmas. Do you have plans?"

Theo found himself opening and shutting his mouth again. There was no reason he should think that he and Wendy had plans. They hadn't *made* actual plans. He just assumed that they were together now, that everything from here out was cozy and domestic. He'd run the gauntlet of her family for Thanksgiving. Of course they'd spend Christmas together. "I don't know," he said honestly. "Probably."

Juliette looked at him quizzically. "Are you seeing someone?" she guessed.

Seeing her. *Feeling* her. Burying himself eagerly inside of her. Laughing with her. "Yes," Theo replied. He certainly wasn't going to apologize for it. "It's pretty new."

"I'm happy for you," Juliette said hastily. "I am. Really. That's great. Do the kids like her?"

"Darius thought she was too weird for me to date,"

Theo said honestly. "He's come around. And Jackson loved her at once. They met when he turned into a gryphon with me for the first time."

"Is she a shifter, then?"

Opening his mouth and shutting it without words seemed to be a theme of this conversation.

"You don't have to tell me," Juliette said, not missing his hesitation.

"She's not," Theo said. "But she feels a bit like one, kind of like Darius. Instinct is really *clear* about her."

Did it sound like a cut on Juliette, implying that instinct hadn't been clear about her? He wasn't going to apologize for that, either.

They were where they were supposed to be, Theo knew without a shred of doubt, and he couldn't regret any of what had brought him to where he was.

Juliette nodded. "That's great. I'm really happy for you." She seemed to gather herself. "I need to get a place for the night."

Theo did apologize then. "I'm sorry, I can't really—"

"No, of course not. It would be too weird. I planned to get a hotel. But I'd like to spend some time with the kids tomorrow. When does Darius get out of school?"

"It's an in-service day," Theo remembered. "Some kind of teacher training. I've got both the kids at home tomorrow."

"That's perfect," Juliette said. "Maybe I can come see them in the morning and you and I can go out for lunch? There's more I'd like to catch up on, but I'm dead on my feet right now."

"It's a date," Theo agreed. "Well, not a date. Just…a lunch."

"Just a lunch," she agreed.

They got to their feet. They each left cash on the table for their drinks.

At the door to the parking lot, as they did their last buttons and zippers before going out into the cold, Juliette said, "You know you can't tell your new girlfriend about this, right?"

Theo felt his hackles rise. "That's not fair. I don't want to do that to Wendy. I don't have any secrets from her and she doesn't have any secrets from me. I won't make that promise."

Juliette looked surprised and taken aback, and Theo realized that he'd stepped forward aggressively and was speaking fiercely.

"You're really serious about her," Juliette said quietly.

"She's the one," Theo said firmly. He didn't apologize for it.

CHAPTER 30

*A*fter Theo left, Wendy wasn't at all ready for sleep and didn't feel like starting a big, messy project, so after a swift shower, she picked one of her in-progress knitting bags and was amused to find that she was halfway through one of the pink hats that Mr. Charles Vissey Smith had objected to so vehemently. That was something she could finish with ease, so she picked a mindless television show and started knitting.

She told herself she wasn't hovering over her phone like a desperate teenager, but she dropped her needles and two stitches when the text alert gave a chime.

It was Addison, to her disappointment, demanding to know if she had another date with Mr. Las Vegas Hotpants yet.

Wendy had to think hard about her answer.

She couldn't exactly say, *Got laid. He's out with Mrs. Ex-Las Vegas Hotpants now.*

She settled for texting an eggplant. Let Addison make of that what she would.

When the phone chimed again before she could pick

up her dropped stitches, she assumed it was Addison demanding more information. Her heart skipped in excitement when she glanced over to see Theo's name on the screen.

She was an independent woman who didn't need a man to make her feel complete. It was ridiculous to be so smitten. Most ridiculous of all, he seemed to be exactly as into her.

I think this is a case where I really should apologize. Can't say much, but it was important news. I wish I could come by and talk, but I have to get back to Darius before my curfew.

Wendy spent a few moments agonizing over what response would make her seem the most composed and not needy or juvenile. Then she decided that maybe it wouldn't be the worst thing if Theo knew she wanted more of him, and the ship had long ago sailed on trying to fool him into thinking she was a serious adult.

Just talk? she typed. She added an eggplant.

I'd DEFINITELY like to come by for more eggplant, Theo agreed with encouraging speed. He added a few fire icons, and, for some reason, a flamingo.

Before Wendy could decide how to reply, smiling in smug satisfaction, another message flickered up.

I don't want you to think I'm not taking you srsly, he texted.

I'm not getting back with Juliette and i don't want you to worry about that for a moment. It's a little complicated, but there's nothing romantic going on there.

Wendy felt relieved.

I'm glad, she typed back. *I'm a one eggplant, one peach kind of woman.*

You're my only peach, Theo assured her.

Wendy laughed even harder when Addison's message flashed at the top of the screen. *?!?!*

Lunch tomorrow? Wendy suggested to Theo. *Eggplant sandwich?*

Three dots flashed up on the screen, disappeared, reappeared, disappeared, and reappeared. Just as Wendy was trying to figure out if she should make a less vague suggestion, there was a text: *I agreed to have lunch with Juliette.*

Immediately after: *She's leaving the day after tomorrow, I have more questions for her.*

And then: *I'm sorry.*

Wendy found an icon of a glass of water and sent that.

She followed it with a quick, *Srsly, I get it. Maybe later this week.*

There was a pause and Wendy wondered if that was the end of it all. She got another two rows knitted terribly and had to go back six stitches for one that she'd dropped.

Bedtime. One son molting. The other is too cool for toothpaste.

Good luck! she replied.

Good night, he answered.

Wendy wasn't sure she'd be able to sleep after that, but the dopamine from sex was a wonderful thing, and her sheets smelled deliciously like Theo and home.

CHAPTER 31

*J*ackson woke early and teleported himself directly into Theo's bed. Theo scolded him gently, then cuddled the fluffy chick against his chest until Jackson fell back into a light slumber as a baby boy. Theo drowsed, cradling him close, and wished his phone was in reach so he could see if Wendy had texted again.

Theo didn't think it was just sexual release that made him feel so relaxed for the first time in several weeks. Everything was working out perfectly. He had answers to all of Juliette's mysterious warnings of danger, which seemed distant and far-off now. Darius seemed to have warmed up to Wendy, Jackson adored her, and...Theo's thoughts drifted to holding her in his arms and calling her Mrs. Royal.

The peace was shattered by Darius's alarm clock, which had apparently not been shut off for the in-service day, and the boy got up and fumbled noisily around in the bathroom. Jackson woke up again and began to fuss, so Theo sighed and got up to feed him and find him a diaper.

"Your mom's coming over later this morning," Theo reminded Darius, when he came into the kitchen to find Darius pouring a bowl of cereal wearing nothing but boxers and a T-shirt. "Please wear clothing."

"I know," Darius groused. "I'm not a baby."

"How's the wrist?" Theo wanted to know. "You're not wearing your brace."

Darius shrugged without answering and rubbed the arm in question.

Despite that inauspicious beginning, breakfast was cheerful. Theo was in too good a mood to let Darius dampen it, and his joviality was contagious. Jackson merrily remained human through the meal, and Darius groaned at Theo's dad jokes and tossed back his own.

They loaded the dishwasher together afterwards, and tidied the house. Theo found himself comparing everything about it to Wendy's cozy place. Where would they live, he wondered. Would they be a strange modern couple and keep two places? Or was there a possibility of a mashup of both of their houses, big enough for his family and her? Maybe with an attached garage that could be her studio…

He was still daydreaming about that future and joking with Darius about pants when Juliette knocked.

"I'll get it," Darius offered, suddenly sober.

Theo was worried that it would be tense and awful. Darius might be mad at Juliette for not being around for him, and Jackson could treat her like a stranger.

But Jackson gave a shriek of delight when he caught sight of her, pulled himself up on the couch, and then face-planted trying to run to her. Darius deftly swooped down to pick him up and tickle him to laughter, and everything was joyful chaos and warm reunion.

Darius talked more than Theo had ever heard him,

sharing stories about school and his play rehearsal. "Tiny Tim's actual name is Timothy, and he's new in town and getting over some kind of horrible illness so he walks with a cane, but he's really cool and has an amazing phone and Dad said he might get me a phone and I'm doing really well in all my classes except English because Mrs. Teddly really hates me…"

"Mrs. Teddly doesn't hate you," Theo corrected. "She just thinks you need to focus."

Juliette coaxed more stories out of him while they played nonsensical games with Jackson stacking blocks and sorting stuffies, all four of them sitting on the carpet together.

It was easy, being a family for a while, and Theo had to sit back and examine his feelings. He had loved Juliette, and he couldn't be sorry for what they'd made, but he kept comparing their interactions with his feelings about Wendy. Wendy felt more like a partner than Juliette ever had.

When Jackson began to rub his eyes and get grumpy, Darius volunteered, "I can make us lunch and put him down for a nap. I know you guys wanted to get out and talk grown-up stuff."

Theo felt his chest swell. "You're a great kid," he said proudly.

Darius looked pleased but also mortified. "Oh, Dad. Don't get weird."

Juliette gave him a big hug, kissed his forehead, and ruffled his hair. "Thanks, sweetie. I'm going to go back to my hotel to do some work after lunch, but I'll be back for dinner."

Darius made a show of smoothing his hair back down. "Whatever."

Jackson gave a shriek of protest as Theo and Juliette put their coats on, but Darius immediately promised him a cheese sandwich and a toy and distracted him while they slipped out.

Theo was glad that Jackson had teleported that morning. It could be exhausting, and it was unlikely that he'd do it again that same day.

He and Juliette went back to the same place they'd met the day before, not for the quality of the bar food, but for the privacy.

"So, about Wendy," Juliette said, after they'd placed their orders.

How do I explain Wendy? Theo wondered. "Did you get permission from your mystery agency for me to tell her?"

"No," Juliette said with a shake of her head. "But I get the feeling that won't stop you. I just want to know a little more about her."

She is our mate, his gryphon said with complete satisfaction. *What more does she need to know?*

"She works at the DMV," Theo said. "She's an amazing painter. She's funny and smart and doesn't care what people think about her. I'm...thinking about asking her to marry me."

He hadn't really intended to admit that. He'd asked Juliette to marry her when she was pregnant with Darius, but hadn't really been sorry when they decided to keep things unofficial.

"That's great," Juliette said sincerely. "I'm really happy for you, Theo. I knew you'd land on your feet."

"We should talk about our...arrangements," Theo said uncomfortably. "And I want to know more about what I should look out for regarding your shifter hunters. Who can I contact if there's a problem?"

Lunch was a rather somber affair, but they hashed out many dull details. "I've got child support arranged through the agency," Juliette said, and Theo was rather astonished at the amounts she named. They'd shared custody of Darius in Las Vegas, and declared it even when they each had a child to care for, but now that Theo had both of the kids, she was prepared to put a portion of her wages to supporting them.

"You make more than I realized," he said wryly. "Being a spy must pay well."

Juliette looked abashed. "Look, Theo, I'm really sorry…"

Theo smirked, looking at his glass of water.

"I wanted to tell you what I did," she said regretfully. "Keeping it from you was probably the hardest part of my job."

Theo realized with a jolt that if she *had* told him while they were together…they might still be together and he'd never have met Wendy. "It worked out," he said in wonder. "It worked out just like it was supposed to." Something occurred to him. "Do I have to sign a non-disclosure? Because we know, are we more at risk now?"

"The agency keeps risk dispersed," Juliette said confidently. "I'll be your sole point of contact and if I ever fall out of touch or you have concerns, this is the card for our cover company in Las Vegas. Ask about the balcony to get past the front desk."

"Juliette, on the balcony?" Theo said thoughtfully. "Very romantic."

"Romeo, wherefore art thou," Juliette teased lightly.

"I hope you find your Romeo," Theo said sincerely.

She looked at him with a curious expression on her face that Theo couldn't identify, then finished the last bites of her tough chicken-fried steak without comment.

They split the bill and left cash. *Going dutch,* Theo thought, remembering the day he'd met Wendy.

He wasn't sure what they were supposed to do as they

left the restaurant and parted at their vehicles. A hug didn't seem right, a handshake felt cold. In the end, he just said, "See you tonight for dinner," and got into his truck.

He had to get right out again after starting it, to scrape the ice from the windshield, and he did the same for Juliette's car because all she had was a credit card and her mittens.

"Thanks, Theo," she said gratefully. "See you tonight."

It could have been worse, Theo decided, driving home. It could have been a horrible, contentious split, fighting over every penny, involving lawyers, and arguing about custody and visitations. They might have tried to poison the kids against each other, or resented the time they wasted together. Theo had so many of the answers now that he'd always wanted...and all the bad feelings were washed away in good memories that he felt like he could enjoy again.

A feeling of unease swept over him, alarming and strong. He'd been so wrapped up in thinking about Juliette and Wendy and the complexity of his life that he hadn't recognized the little thread of instinct underneath, suggesting...what, it wasn't clear, but that agitation was swelling into anxiousness now.

Theo thought he knew what it meant on the drive home when a white SUV came screeching recklessly out of his cul-de-sac and nearly sideswiped his truck. He scowled back over his shoulder at it, trying to make out the plate numbers so that he could call in and report them. It was dangerous driving like that in a neighborhood full of kids. He was lucky instinct had him on alert or he might have gotten hit himself.

They were California plates, and Theo got just a few of the digits committed to memory. To his surprise, instinct hadn't calmed, and it continued to thrum in him after the danger of the crash had passed.

He was surprised to see tracks in the driveway that weren't his own truck tracks, and Theo rushed to the house, his worry growing. The front door wasn't locked, and Theo made a mental note to remind Darius that he should do that when he was home alone with Jackson. He didn't want to call out, because Jackson was probably sleeping, but his alarm escalated when Darius didn't come to greet him.

"Darius," he said, tapping on the boy's door. "Darius?"

He opened it in a rush and animals gave little startled cries and chirps, but Darius wasn't there. With no care for quiet, Theo hollered, "Darius? Jackson?"

The house was empty. The crib was empty. There was no note on the table, and Jackson's diaper bag and Darius's coat were still hanging by the door.

His kids were *gone*.

endy thought that it was pretty amazing what getting laid could do for her attitude.

She'd been stuck in the checkout line at the deli for nearly thirty minutes of her precious lunch break because the cashier was in training and her supervisor had abandoned her. When it was finally Wendy's turn to pay, she assured the girl that she'd done her best and that it would get easier.

"The first week on my job at the DMV, I deleted a month's worth of personal records. They could restore them from backups, but it took the entire day and let me tell you, I felt just like you are now. Think of it this way, you're going to get through this day, and it's only going to be better from here."

The girl nearly wept. "Thank you," she said gratefully. "I mean that. Thank you. It's nice to find someone with… something in common."

Did she say that a little pointedly? Wendy wondered if she was a shifter, trying to puzzle out Wendy's confusing signal. It wasn't like a shifter tingle, but it wasn't *not* like one, and on another day, the conversation would have reminded Wendy that she was broken and lacking.

Today?

Today, Wendy was whole, all by herself in her head.

She was everything she needed to be, and she left the store feeling like maybe she'd done something worthwhile. It was easy to be cheerful and supportive when her whole body felt like it was happily humming, like it was all put together the way it was supposed to be at last.

It had been a long time since she'd felt this relaxed.

Wendy pulled her phone out of her pocket halfway across the parking lot a moment before it started ringing, not sure how she knew it would, and wondered why Theo's number on her screen gave her a moment of stomach-dropping alarm instead of just excitement.

There was no reason to think that something was wrong, but something in her gut was sure that it was. "What is it?" she blurted when she accepted the call.

"Jackson and Darius," Theo said, the tone in his voice confirming the irrational feeling she'd had. "They're gone."

"Gone?" Wendy tried to make sense of it. "They ran away?"

"Kidnapped, I think. Juliette says there's this scientific corporation that knows about shifters, that's been studying them, maybe dissecting them, I don't know! I just got home and the front door is unlocked. There are truck tracks in the snow on the driveway." He lowered his voice. "I can't feel them. I can't *go* to them. They must be unconscious." There was understandable panic in his voice.

"That doesn't mean they've been hurt." Wendy threw her bags haphazardly into the back seat of her car. Usually she carefully put the milk and meat on the floor, and was obsessive about making sure that her vegetables and fruit wouldn't bruise on the way home. "What can I do?"

"Can you run plates?" Theo asked. "I passed a car leaving the neighborhood that might have been involved. I got a few of the numbers and a make and model—I mean, it could have come from my house, but I don't know, and I only got a glimpse."

"Of course. I'll be at work in about five minutes. Give me what you've got, anything that will help me narrow it down."

Theo rattled off what he knew and Wendy wrote everything down on her receipt with a half-dead pen. "I'm going to the DMV right now. Do you want to meet me there? Are you okay to drive? Or…?" Should she suggest out loud that he teleport?

"I can drive," Theo said fiercely.

Wendy tried to think about what else someone might do when their kids were kidnapped. "Have you called the cops?"

"What would I tell them?" Theo said. "My kids are magic and bad people kidnapped them for experimentation? I'd have to explain so much. And I keep hoping I'll be able to *go* to them. I think it's just that they're unconscious—I can't teleport to someone who is asleep. But what if something is blocking me? What if they're…?"

"Theo, Theo!" Wendy was shouting into her phone as she put it in the console between the front seats and started her cold car. She had to turn on the defroster on full to clear the frosty windshield. "They're fine. We're going to find them. It's going to be okay! I am driving to the DMV right now and we'll figure something out. Breathe with me, Theo. Breathe with me. Are you breathing? Your brain needs all the oxygen it can get right now, okay?"

"I'm breathing," Theo said, actually sounding more

calm.

"Did you call Juliette?"

"Juliette?"

"Their mother, Theo. How's that breathing thing going?"

"I'm still breathing. I haven't called her yet. I just got here. I called you first. I should do that."

Wendy was pretty sure that it meant something that Theo had called her first, and not the mother of his children. "I'm going to hang up on you now, Theo, and you're going to call her and then you're going to drive to the DMV, okay? Please do not talk to her while you are driving because you are having enough trouble with the thinking and the respiration at the same time, do you hear me? One hard thing at a time."

"I'll call her," Theo promised, "then I'll drive. And I'll breathe. And I'll think."

"You've got this, Theo. They're going to wake up and you'll be able to find them and it's all going to be okay and I love you."

There was silence in return and for a moment, Wendy hoped he'd hung up and not heard her stupid, impulsive, ridiculous confession. They weren't to the point of declarations of love yet. They'd had a few hot kisses and, yeah, absolutely mind-blowing sex, but that wasn't a reason to say *love* things.

"I love you too," he said then.

Wendy's whole being seemed to light up, and she felt tears sting her eyes. Maybe it wasn't too soon? Maybe this crazy feeling in her heart was right. Maybe she was worth loving. She dragged a mitten across her face. "Call Juliette! Drive! Breathe! Be careful!"

This time she made sure that he hung up, and then she decided that breathing was good advice for her, too.

CHAPTER 33

Theo pulled up at the DMV as Wendy was unlocking the door, and she paused with her keys in the lock to throw her arms around him. "It's going to be okay," she murmured. "We'll find them."

Theo soaked what comfort he could from her embrace, but it wasn't much. Right now, the only lead they had was a few numbers of a California license and a description of the vehicle. When he tried to reach out to teleport to Darius, he just felt a blankness, like he wasn't *anywhere*. "Juliette said she'd call her...agency. She's a secret agent. A spy. She didn't want me to tell you, but I told her I was going to anyway. She's on her way."

"I don't know if I'll be able to narrow this down to something useful," Wendy said skeptically, as she booted up her computer. She didn't even bother taking off her coat before she settled down to work. "But let's see what we can find. We've got a make and model and color and I can try a few wildcards"

Theo paced in the lobby on the other side of her desk and wished he could look over her shoulder. He cast continuously for Darius, hoping for some sense of him, any hint that he could reach across space for him. Darius. Jackson. His boys. The most precious part of his world. He peeled off his coat and threw it onto one of the lobby chairs.

How could they be gone? He was ready to tear someone apart for threatening them, and the most he could do was kick a heavy stanchion and regret it with his toes.

"Oh," Wendy said after a moment.

"Oh?" Theo almost vaulted over her desk. What did *Oh* mean?

"There are about a hundred options," she said hesitantly, "but the chances of this being one of them by coincidence is like *nil*."

Theo wanted to reach across and strangle her, he was so worked up. "Who?!"

"Owen Davis."

"Who is that? And why do I care?"

"Owen Davis is Addison's ex-boyfriend. He was a controlling dirtbag who kept her under his thumb for way too long and took it really personally when she left him. He followed her here to Montana from California and I thought that he'd given up, but...maybe he hadn't."

"What does this have to do with my kids?" Theo wanted to know. He and his gryphon were laser focused on the issue at hand.

"More than you might think," Wendy said. "Addison told me that Veronica was the one who told Owen where to find her, and I'm pretty sure that Veronica has big suspicions about shifters. If Owen knows—or thinks he knows —about shifters, and he wants revenge on my cousin for escaping him, it's at least possible that he's working with people trying to uncover their secrets. I don't think it's just by chance that his is one of the possible licenses to come up in this search!"

"Where is he? How do I find him?"

"It's a California license," Wendy said. "I can get a phone number for him, and his home address in that state, but if he's in Nickel City, that's not going to help us track him down now."

"Can't you trace his cellphone?" Theo demanded.

"This is the DMV," Wendy reminded him. "I'm not the police."

They both turned in alarm when the door jangled and Theo relaxed a tiny bit to realize that it was Juliette, not a stranger, striding in.

"What happened? Where are the kids?" Juliette gave Wendy a deeply suspicious look over the counter and started to draw Theo away.

"This is Wendy," Theo said, resisting her. "She knows *everything*."

Juliette's gaze flickered back to Wendy, skeptical, and Theo bristled in defense.

Before he could make any move to interfere, Wendy was standing up and thrusting her hand across the counter. "You must be Juliette," she said, shaking her hand. "Oh my gosh, you're *gorgeous*. Theo says you're a secret agent, but I'm probably not supposed to say that out loud. Well, here we are anyway, and I think we've got a lead, but it's not a lot to go on."

She turned the monitor around to give them a look at the screen without giving Juliette a chance to reply.

"This is the kind of SUV that belongs to my cousin's awful ex, he's from California, and he's got kind of a grudge thing going on, so it seems possible—even *likely*— that he's involved. Addison never told him she was a shifter, but he did see some things she wishes he hadn't and he's not dumb, even if he's a jerk, so it's likely that he's put some pieces together and fallen in with your bad guys. He was probably part of snatching your kids, do you think he'd try to leave straight for Las Vegas?"

Juliette stared at Wendy for a moment in awe, but rallied quickly. "It's more likely that he'd stash the kids somewhere temporary close by and make sure they didn't have a tail, then move them later when they were sure that they hadn't been followed. These guys are good at what they do."

"Hmm," Wendy said. "Okay, if that's the case, we have to catch Owen and shake the details out of him before he leaves town."

"You said we don't have a way to track him," Theo said. He still wanted to tear something in half.

"We don't have a way to track him," Wendy agreed, "but maybe we can draw him here. Oh, yeah! I can get his driver's license revoked and tell him he needs to have it fixed right now. He won't risk driving a car full of abducted kids with a revoked driver's license between here and Vegas."

"You can do that?"

"The state of Montana can revoke out-of-state licenses if they get enough traffic violations. This is technically above my paygrade," Wendy said with a wiggle of her eyebrows. "But my boss leaves her passwords on a sticky note on her monitor, so I can make it happen. Let's do this!" She rocketed out of her chair and dashed for the back room.

"She's really *something*," Juliette murmured.

Theo wasn't sure how she meant it. "She's amazing," he said protectively.

Juliette put both hands up. "I didn't intend it as a cut. She'd be a great agent, if she's interested in moving on from the DMV. She's…just not what I thought your type was."

"She's not like you," Theo agreed. "And I don't mean that as a cut."

Juliette could have taken that several ways, Theo realized as he said it, and he watched those several ways cross her face. It settled into grudging respect. "You didn't apologize," she pointed out.

Theo was confused for a moment. "Should I?"

Juliette smiled. "No, it's just that…it used to be your default. It's admirable to shoulder everything, but it feels like you've accepted that not everything is your fault and you don't owe everyone in the world more than you can give."

Had he done that with her? Was that why their relationship had failed? Theo realized in astonishment that he could look back at it clearly for the first time…and it didn't matter whose fault it was. It didn't matter that he'd made mistakes, or she had. He was here, now, making the life that he had the best that he could, and there didn't have to be blame or anger or ugly feelings about what had already happened.

And he certainly had more important things to deal with now. His kids were still missing, and he still couldn't sense Darius or Jackson to teleport to them.

CHAPTER 34

"Mr. Owen Davis? This is—" Wendy just kept herself from giving her name. It was too small a town for him not to know that Wendy at the DMV was Addison's cousin. Wendy wasn't *that* common a name. "—the Nickel City DMV calling to let you know that your current California driver's license has been suspended due to multiple local speeding violations. We'll need you to pay for those violations or file a dispute in person at a DMV office within 24 hours to continue using your license. It will be unlawful to drive with your license suspended."

"What?!"

Channeling her very best Veronica Chase voice, Wendy loftily continued. "We are open today until five PM. Drive safe!"

She hung up before Owen could do more than sputter, not wanting to complicate the situation unnecessarily. Lying could get messy, and she didn't want to have to remember a story later.

She immediately dialed Addison on her personal phone.

"Addy, listen up. Theo's kids have been kidnapped, and it looks like Owen is involved. He's working with some kind of scientific foundation in Nevada that has been researching shifters, and I'm pretty sure he knows what you and Gabby and Roderick are, and probably where you are."

Wendy heard Addison suck in a breath on the other end of the line. "Are we in immediate danger?"

"I don't know. But if he knows about you, he might know about Tiny Paws and the other kids. He's been seen with Veronica Chase."

"And Veronica Chase asked Olivia about local wildlife photos," Addison said flatly.

"I saw her talking with Mr. Charles Vissey Smith."

"Who?"

"A local conspiracy weirdo."

"Is he part of this?"

"I doubt it," Wendy said. "But Veronica Chase giving a nutball like that the time of day seemed remarkable enough to note."

"It's pretty odd," Addison agreed. "Ok, what do you want us to do?"

Wendy was used to taking point in childish games and things that didn't matter, not life-and-death, children-kidnapping, bad-guys-with-grudges stuff. "Um," she said inelegantly. "Well, I've got Owen coming to the DMV on a trumped up traffic fine thing because we figured he's our best lead for finding Jackson and Darius. And…we could use backup, maybe? Theo's here, but Owen might bring friends and…"

"…You want to have more friends."

Addison seemed to be taking this remarkably well. There was a tone of resignation in her voice, like she'd known this was coming.

Maybe she had. Shifters had always had to face how difficult it was going to be to keep their secrets with the swell of cheap and available recording technology. As ubiquitous as cellphones were now, it was a minor miracle that they hadn't *already* been exposed. And Addison always feared that Owen wasn't quite done with her, personally.

And this time, Wendy wasn't on the sidelines because she wasn't one of them. She was in the thick of the coming battle.

"I think that Theo is ready to take him on single-clawed, and his ex is here, but I'd like to stack the odds in my favor."

"His ex?"

"It's complicated."

Addison spoke to the side, her words just muffled enough not to make out, and Wendy heard Cherry's reply in the same way.

"I'll be there in twenty minutes."

"I wouldn't want you to leave the day care undefended," Wendy said. "Should you stay there?"

"Owen is my problem," Addison said grimly. "And I'm calling in the big guns to take my place."

"Big guns?" Wendy said avidly. There were *big guns?*

"I know a *dragon.*"

That was a *very* big gun. A deeply comforting big gun.

Wendy returned to the DMV lobby to find Juliette deep in conversation with Theo, and she had a stab of jealousy. They were intimately close, talking privately, and Wendy was keenly aware of how put-together Juliette was, how classically beautiful and competent she seemed. Wendy might have a basket of eclectic skills, but knitting wasn't going to be of much use right now, and Juliette was a super spy badass. Wendy felt soft and useless as she walked around the counter out into the lobby.

Then Theo looked up and saw her. Wendy braced for his guilt. He was such a nice guy, he'd feel bad for liking his gorgeous, competent ex more than his new maybe-girlfriend who was great with forms.

But his expression was only joy. "I can feel Darius again!" he said, rising to meet her eagerly with not even a sideways glance for Juliette. "Instinct says I can get to him now, I was about to come tell you!"

"That's great!" Wendy said, not having to dredge deep to feel happiness for him.

"It could be a trap," Juliette warned. She rose gracefully to her feet. "Let's take my car. I've got weapons."

Theo ignored her and took the time to gather Wendy up into his arms and give her a quick, desperate hug while Juliette turned away in embarrassment. Wendy could feel him trembling as she grasped him back and realized that he was afraid. She did her best to pour her hope and support back into him through their embrace. "You'll find them," she promised, and she was surprised to find that there was a pressure inside of her that seemed to think he would. "Everything is going to be okay."

Theo stepped back and sucked in his breath, then turned and Wendy watched all of the muscles in his neck bunch up like he was lifting something impossibly heavy, and he seemed to step into an invisible puddle of water, disappearing as if he was stepping through a rippling surface.

She had watched Theo teleport once before, out of her kitchen with Jackson, but it was different watching him step into nothing at all, knowing that he was going into some unknown danger.

It's okay, something seemed to whisper to her. This was the right thing for him to do, even if Wendy ached to see him go.

Juliette turned back from the poster just in time to see him vanish and Wendy realized from her expression that she hadn't known about that particular skill set.

"Oh, yeah," Wendy said as casually as she could manage. "He teleports, too."

She only realized then that she hadn't told Theo that Owen was on his way.

CHAPTER 35

Theo felt the world go away as he fixed his attention on his destination. He concentrated on Darius, keying on their bond. The boy felt fuzzy, and Theo guessed that he was still fighting off some kind of drug, but he gradually swam into focus like Theo was adjusting a telescope. His oldest son, such a source of frustration and pride. He thought about Darius when he was the size of Jackson, toddling around, learning how to be a person. He thought about what a great kid Darius was now, how selfless and clever he could be. He had to get to Darius, and keep his human form, and take the step that would go between one place and miles away, without thinking too hard about how it all worked or if he might fail.

He felt his gryphon snap his beak as if he was cutting through the fabric of reality and everything swept away in a senseless moment of nothing. He stepped blindly through and felt it rip away behind him as he came out into a dark room.

A quick glance around told Theo that it was a storage unit or a shipping container, roughly converted into a bedroom with a cot piled in blankets and a throw rug as a nod to comfort. There were two low file cabinets with a piece of plywood over the top as a make-shift desk. The office chair was surprisingly high quality. He could hear the muffled sounds of big equipment nearby. Were they in the Tails? Maybe at the railyard? It was too bad teleporting didn't come with GPS. He'd forgotten his phone in his coat pocket at the DMV.

"—ad!" Darius was hurtling into Theo's side. "I knew you'd come." Was he crying?

Theo wasn't going to embarrass him if he was. "I will always come," he said fiercely, wrapping arms around his son. When had he gotten so tall? "Always." He didn't consider the time that they stood in a warm embrace wasted in the slightest, but he couldn't linger as long as he wanted to enjoy the moment of Darius's rare vulnerability.

"Where's Jackson?"

"Here, he's here." Darius pulled away, dragging an arm across his face, and pointed at the bed. "I think they drugged us with something."

As if Theo needed another needle for his rage.

Jackson was sleeping as a gryphon, tucked into a fluffy ball. Theo had mistaken him for a pillow at first glance. He was breathing evenly and sleeping no more deeply than he usually did. When Theo put a hand on his side, he clacked his beak and tucked his wings in more tightly.

Theo stood to investigate their prison. They weren't in immediate danger, he decided.

The storage container wasn't set up as a cell, exactly; it seemed like a temporary office. Had Juliette's evil scientist corporation set up a station in Nickel City? How much did they know? The filing cabinets were locked, but weren't of strong enough construction to stand up to shifter fury. Theo yanked the first drawer out with sheer force. Jackson gave a little growl of discontent at the noise, and Darius went to scoop him up and comfort him.

"Tell me what happened," Theo said, thumbing through the tabs. Not that he expected to find a handy supervillain address book, but he was hoping for some clues about where they were and who had done this. Something they could use in a legal court. But it only looked like real estate documents and utility bills.

"I'd just finished Jackson's bath," Darius said. "I was letting him feed Ginger—through the cage. It was totally safe!—and I heard someone pull up in the driveway. I didn't really think anything about it. Maybe they were turning around. Or maybe it was a package, and they'd leave it on the porch. But they knocked."

"You didn't open the door for them."

"Of *course* not." Darius sounded more stressed than outraged. "I was just going to ignore it, but there was a kind of a scratching noise at the lock and I heard the deadbolt open. I thought it might be you, but it wasn't your truck and I heard voices that definitely weren't you. I tried to hide Jackson, but he turned into a gryphon and I was like *oh shi—oh crud*—and there were these guys in black with flashlights and I heard a shot but it was sort of more like woosh than a bang and then I was waking up here."

"You did fine," Theo said, hoping to ease some of Darius's distress. "There wasn't anything else you could do."

"Is the zoo okay? They didn't kidnap any of my pets, did they?"

Theo had a moment of humor imaging scientists puzzling over Darius's perfectly ordinary animals. "They were all fine," he assured his son.

Outside the door, there was a sudden commotion of voices and banging, muffled by the hefty door. It occurred to Theo with a sinking heart that there might be cameras somewhere. A swift inspection of the ceiling revealed several devices that might be surveillance.

Wendy. He had to get back to Wendy *now*.

We could fight them, his gryphon suggested. *They stole our chicks.*

Theo would have loved to do battle with the people who had tried to take his children, but he wasn't willing to risk them, either. He took a hasty and random handful of files. "We need to get out of here."

"Can you get both of us back?" Darius asked. "Because if you can't, you should take Jackson."

As brave as Darius was being, Theo had no intention of leaving him behind.

Theo had brought people with him through his portal before, but it was hard, like he was dragging an unwilling dog with him on a leash. A really big dog with its paws dug in, trying to resist and shake out of its collar. He'd never done it with two before, even if one of them was Jackson's size.

It was somewhat easier to teleport as a gryphon, so Theo shifted, taking the files he was holding. If there were cameras in the room, they had already seen Jackson, and they'd seen him rip through space right into their secure facility. Theo had nothing left to hide from them. He folded his wings tight against his back and nudged at Darius until he figured out the plan.

"You want me to ride you?"

Proximity would make it easier. Darius gathered Jackson tighter and stood skeptically next to Theo. As a gryphon, Theo was as high at the shoulder as the top of Darius's head; he filled the room and felt his tail lashing against the wall behind him. Theo knelt and Darius scrambled on top of him, one hand clutching Jackson close.

"This would really be cool if, you know, we weren't running for our lives."

There were shouts outside the door now, and the scratch of metal. The shipping container had big lever latches, and Theo heard them start to creak.

Theo concentrated as hard as he could, using the same mental mantra that brought his clothing with him when he shifted as he cast his mind towards Wendy. *Is it safe?* he asked his gryphon. He wasn't going to risk his children if the whole idea was misguided.

I think it is, his gryphon said reluctantly. *It will be a lot.*

Instinct was an awareness at the back of his head, nudging him on, but not strongly. Something wasn't quite aligned yet.

Wendy. He thought fixedly of Wendy, of her curly hair and her easy laugh. The way she flaunted society's expectations. That underlying vulnerability because she so desperately wanted to be liked despite her self-declared independence. He could feel her, across all the distance between them, like a brilliant lighthouse of her powerful energy guiding them home. She was his anchor.

The latch mechanism groaned as someone started to open the storage box and there were shouts outside. He was running out of time. Darius was settled on his back, leaning forward with one hand clutching at Theo's feathers and the other wrapped around Jackson. "I don't know what to hold on to!" he cried.

Theo would just have to move carefully, not jostle them off. He was concentrating all of his attention on Wendy, on the draw back to Nickel City, about how she felt to his soul, and he felt her connect perfectly with him, clicking into place as instinct swelled.

Now! Go!

Theo surged to his feet and went forward, tearing the space all around them.

It was terrible, and took twice as long as a usual teleport, unable to feel or see or hear anything, desperate to keep Darius and Jackson on his back, but not sure if he was. If he stumbled, or lost them in the transport— He had to stop thinking about that and focus again on Wendy, on the draw of Wendy across space and maybe even time, on the strength of her, the solid realness that could draw them all back. She wouldn't waste time dwelling on fears and worries. She would do the things that needed done, and she would do them her best and she would do them so kindly and Theo wanted that in his life more than anything else he could imagine.

He was still nowhere, still between places, and it felt like they must be lost. Would they wander forever in nothing? Had he doomed them all?

I'm so sorry…

*Stop apologizing and come **here**.* It was Wendy's voice, and Theo wasn't sure if it was real, or if he'd just imagined it because it was exactly what she would say, and he was finally stepping out into real space again and Darius was slipping off him, yelling and pulling feathers out of Theo's neck and trying to cradle Jackson as he fell.

CHAPTER 36

The door chimed and Wendy looked hopefully over before she remembered that Theo would probably not be using the front door and it was still too early to expect Addison.

Her heart dropped.

Owen Davis looked exactly like Wendy remembered from Addison's photos. He was handsome in that *I-know-it* way, and he had an easy smile and wore nice clothing.

Looks could be deceiving. He had kept Addison all but a captive for years, subtly abusing and controlling her. He was that clever kind of cruel that never looked particularly dangerous or was ever overtly controlling. He could put on company manners that were deeply convincing, and had a plethora of natural charm and charisma.

But Wendy wasn't fooled, and she didn't think that it was just because she knew Addison's story. It was like there was a radiation detector inside of her that was clicking like crazy. *Bad, wrong, danger!*

Wendy told herself that it was only her imagination. She knew what Owen was capable of, and that was all that was getting her hackles up now. It was nothing supernatural, and she was alone in her own head.

She shot Juliette a glance of warning and picked up a paper from the desk at random. "Here!" she said brightly. "This might be what you're looking for!"

Juliette did a much better job than Wendy of keeping any feeling from her face. Wendy actually worried that she hadn't caught the message until she saw Juliette's hand flashing her a thumbs up from the far side of her body where Owen couldn't see it.

Everything seemed very loud in the quiet room. The "Employees-only" half-door to get behind her desk squealed like a rusty cattle gate, and her chair casters were noisier than ever as Wendy settled into her seat.

Owen glanced at Juliette, who was innocently studying the form for tractor title transfers that Wendy had pressed on her. "Go ahead," Juliette said to Owen with a careless shrug. "I'm not ready yet." She turned away and sat down in one of the lobby chairs.

Wendy tried to imitate Juliette's casual air. "What can I help you with?" she asked as Owen approached her station.

"I got a call about my license being suspended for multiple violations and I just need to get that all straightened out."

"Have you—?"

Owen's voice was deceptively reasonable. "I've already looked it up online and it's definitely been restricted. I need to talk to your manager and get this all fixed. I'm sure that won't be any problem."

He gave Wendy a winning smile.

One of Owen's most dangerous features was that he was *smart*. Most mean guys were also clunkers in the mental department, but Owen was not only deeply cruel, but terribly clever. Addison had been helpless in his grip not because he was overtly possessive, but because he could be subtle in his manipulation and relentless in his obsession.

Did he recognize her as Addison's cousin? Wendy thought it was very likely that he had enough pieces of information to put that all together, but she wasn't sure if Owen would think anything of it. She was just a DMV state employee doing her job. Pay no attention to the nameplate on the counter. She wished she'd thought to cover it before he got there.

"Let's see what we're looking at. Your license, please?" Wendy stuck to her script. "Mr. Owen Davies?" She mispronounced his last name, then wondered if she was laying it on too thick when Juliette gave her a quick look of warning.

Wendy drew the license number up on the computer screen. "Oh yes, I see. The state of Montana issued this revocation just this week. You have seven moving violations here in Nickel City."

"That's impossible," Owen scoffed. He was still being jovial, but there was an edge to his voice.

"Well, it's certainly an impressive record," Wendy said, matching his light tone. "Traffic fines are based on how far you were over the speed limit, and it looks like you have a balance due of seven hundred and ninety dollars. Tsk. One of these was in a school zone!"

"I haven't been pulled over once since I got here," Owen protested.

"These appear to be automated traffic speeding tick-ets," Wendy said airily. "It's amazing what technology can do these days!"

"But I wasn't notified of any until just today," Owen said, with a sharper edge of impatience.

"Notices are sent within seventy-two hours of violation to the address of record." Wendy explained with a sunny smile. "Have you checked your mail?"

Owen gave her a narrow-eyed look, and Wendy wondered if she was being *too* cheerful. "Would you prefer to file a dispute? It might take as much as two weeks to resolve, as it has to go through the district office in Butte."

She didn't trust his sudden whiplash mood switch when his mouth slid into a smooth smile. "That would be lovely. Thank you so much, *Wendy*. You've been *such* a big help to me."

There was an unmistakable sense of unease uncurling in Wendy's chest. She was in *trouble*.

The lobby door gave a chime then, and Wendy looked past to see Addison. She was alone, no sign of any big guns, and the spark of worry in Wendy's chest turned into a raging flame as Owen turned to see her, too.

When Owen reached into his coat, it might have just been to get a phone, or his wallet, but Wendy suddenly knew, like there was a voice in her head, shouting *Duck!*

Wendy was so surprised she almost didn't, but something seemed to take over her limbs and she was flinging herself out of her chair as Owen unholstered a gun and fired exactly where she'd been sitting.

"I bet that being a shapeshifter doesn't protect you from bullets, *witch!*" he shouted.

Wendy was wedged beneath her desk, not even entirely sure where her limbs were. Everything seemed bright and slow, and she knew the particle board of her workstation wouldn't protect her if Owen fired through it. Her only chance was that he didn't know exactly where she was. How many shots did that kind of gun have? Wendy had no idea.

And Addison was out there, unarmed, and Owen was

still pissed that she'd had the gall to leave him, even if he blamed Wendy for helping her get away.

"Owen, don't be stupid!" Wendy hollered, staying out of sight.

"Hey," Juliette was saying smoothly. "There's no reason to fly off the handle."

"Owen, what are you doing?!"

"Are you all freaks?" Owen wanted to know.

"There's no reason to point that at me," Juliette said, her voice as calm as ever. "I don't know what you're talking about."

"Oh, I think you do, Juliette Catellier." Owen said.

Addison gave a squeak of fear and Wendy guessed Owen had pointed the gun at her. "You don't want to *hurt* anyone, Owen!" she said desperately.

Wendy wasn't so sure about that. The gunshot was still loud in her ears, and her heart was pounding in her chest.

Owen had been humiliated and rejected, and he wasn't the kind of guy who was going to let that go easily. It looked like he had finally snapped.

"The whole world is going to know about you freaks and mutants," Owen said. "You can't keep it a secret. You'll all be put in cages, where you belong, where you can't hurt people or use your magical powers to *control* us."

Wendy dared to look up over the top of her desk. She'd been right about him turning the gun on Addison.

The one thing they had going for them was that there were three of them, flanking him from every side, and he couldn't shoot them all at once.

Would he actually shoot Addison? He'd been obsessed with her, absolutely fixated on what he called love.

"You're a fine one to talk about control, Owen," Addison said, her voice shaking.

"You're one of *them!*" Owen spat. "You bewitched me!

I would never have looked twice at a plain little nothing like you. You're dirt! And that boyfriend of yours, he was that wolf, and that puppy you had, probably your filthy spawn. They shouldn't even exist. *You* shouldn't exist. I should have taken care of you before—"

"Stop it, Owen!" Addison was crying, but she looked angry and afraid, more than sad.

"There's no need for this," Juliette was saying, her hands spread wide. "Owen, put down the gun and we'll talk."

Owen swung the gun back to Juliette. "I know about you," he snarled. "You're the human who betrayed your kind. You work for them and aren't any better."

He still hadn't noticed Wendy, and she cast about for some way—any way!—to stop him.

There were no weapons at hand, no handy frying pans or spears, and Wendy had a whimsical moment of wondering if her boss would let her decorate her desk with more useful items in the future.

If she even had a future.

Claws! something suggested in her head. *Teeth!* She tamped that down as a stress-fueled fantasy.

Wendy was sure that she and Juliette and Addison all together could overpower Owen. The problem was the gun. He could shoot at least two of them before they could get him down and disarmed. And she couldn't do anything cowering behind her desk.

She took the only thing she could find with heft, a stapler, in one hand and clambered as quietly as she could up onto the desktop.

Juliette was shaking her head, her lips tight, and although she wasn't looking at Wendy, Owen seemed to sense her behind him.

Wendy froze as Owen turned and his gun swung back

to her. She was crouched on top of her desk, it was too late to go back into hiding, and she was sure that leaping at him now would be suicide.

He was going to shoot her and Juliette would probably be able to overpower him too late, and her boss was going to complain bitterly about all the extra paperwork a death on the job would be. She was going to bleed all over her desk. At least the commercial carpet was supposed to be stain-resistant.

She could hear Addison shouting, distantly, and Juliette was still trying to talk Owen down, and Wendy's heart was pounding in her ears, and there was another voice that was just as loud that didn't make a lick of sense telling her to *freeze, hold still, hang on, just wait!*

Out of the corner of her eye, because she didn't dare to turn her head to look, Wendy saw a gryphon stepping out of nowhere, charging into the DMV lobby with wings spread and beak open in a predatory scream.

Theo!

He was bigger than Wendy had thought he would be, almost as tall as a stallion, with a dangerously hooked beak and wings that filled the lobby and swept every loose paper into motion as he beat them. He was a rich golden color, from his eagle head to his lion hindquarters, and a tufted tail lashed behind him. Darius was sliding off his feathered neck, yelling and cradling a small burden that must be Jackson in one arm.

Owen turned, swinging his gun to meet this new threat, and Wendy didn't stop to think.

She was pretty sure that gryphons weren't impervious to bullets, and Darius was completely vulnerable, and something was screaming in her head to *go now! Protect our mate, bite and claw!*

Wendy launched herself from the top of her desk at

Owen with the stapler and realized right before she hit him that Juliette was doing the same from the other side. Neither of them had time to alter their course before they collided, Owen directly between them.

The gun fired wildly. Wendy wasn't sure which direction it was pointed, or which direction was even up and her heart squeezed in white-hot panic. If Theo had been hit! Or Darius! Or Jackson! Or Addison! Even Juliette! Her head knocked against someone's elbow and she saw stars as she dropped the useless stapler and wrestled to hold on to Owen and keep him from hurting anyone else that she loved.

A screech deafened her, wild and furious, and she was buffeted aside by feathered wings as Theo barreled directly into them.

Wendy wasn't sure if it was relief or terror that burned through her. On the one hand, she was certain that Theo could save her, and on the other, she was petrified that Owen would shoot him point-blank.

Owen stopped struggling in her grip and Wendy dared to open her eyes, not even realizing that she'd closed them.

The gun was knocked clear, and Owen was on his knees, grappled between her and Juliette. Theo had claws on either side of him and he had a wicked, sharp beak open in unmistakable threat. Darius had fallen off and rolled to the side, his arms protectively around Jackson, who thought this was all a very fun game and was shrieking in excitement and trying to squirm out to play.

CHAPTER 37

*S*houts of fear barely registered to Theo's ears and were nothing to the scream of rage that was coming from his eagle throat, his beak snapping inches from Owen's face.

He pinned the man to the ground, buffeting Juliette and Wendy aside with his wings and it was everything he could do not to tear the man limb from limb or sink claws into his guts and pull them out in one easy motion.

It was usually his gryphon keeping him cautious, with words of wisdom and moderation to keep Theo out of trouble too deep. But his gryphon was furious and animal-angry now, absolutely beyond sense or reason. It was Theo who hauled him back from rending Owen on the spot, mindful of his watching sons and Wendy, who shouted, "Don't hurt him! God knows that jerk deserves it, but it will be exactly what people need to believe the worst of shifters!"

How could she have common sense at a time like this?

But even though she was shaking her head in pain and cradling an arm—had Theo hurt *her* with his reckless advance?—she was thinking about the big picture, and dammit, she was right.

If Theo killed Owen now, even if he just ripped the odious man up a little like he wanted to, he was playing right into all the terrible stories of shifters and sorcery that would make the inevitable reveal of magic worse for everyone who had it.

They had to take the high road, disarm him, and… somehow keep him from ever hurting anyone again.

He looked up to find that Addison had picked up Owen's gun. She had it held tight in both hands and she was pointing it directly at her ex. There was a set to her jaw that Theo recognized.

"Let him up," she said firmly, and Theo stepped back with a growl that was part lion and part angry bird.

Owen lay still, not sure if he was being spared.

The entire room took a breath.

Addison's hands trembled.

Theo shifted, dropped the files he was still holding, and straddled Owen, reaching down to grab him by the collar and haul him to his feet. He drew him up directly into his face. "Why should I spare you?" he asked dangerously. "You took my children. You tried to kill my mate. You are a weak and spineless worm who *deserves* to die at my hands."

"I have friends," Owen said desperately. "Powerful friends."

"Veronica Chase?" Wendy said suspiciously.

Owen glanced sideways at her, but Theo didn't give him space to face her. "Better than that," he scoffed. Bluster was probably all he had left at this point. "They're going to find you and take you apart to figure out all your fancy voodoo tricks. Everyone will know about you and you will all be powerless and cast out!"

He glanced the other direction at Addison. "You'll wish you had stayed with me, bi—"

Theo shoved him ungently in the shoulder before he could finish the word. "There are children present."

"Freak children!" Owen retorted. "Mutant kids! You're all aberrations and monsters! You'll be hunted and put down like mad dogs!"

"How did you date this jerk?" Wendy asked Addison. Her voice was the only thing that kept Theo from shifting at his gryphon's insistence that they answer his threats to their children with permanent silence.

Addison gave a shaky laugh. "He's really nice until you get to know him," she said.

Theo shoved Owen into Wendy's desk and was glad to see his eyes widen in sudden terror as he pressed close.

"Don't hurt me," Owen begged. "I take it all back! Let me live!"

He cast his gaze to Addison and Wendy, but if he expected sympathy there, he found none. "I'm sorry!" he howled, clearly in fear of his life.

Theo took more satisfaction from Owen's terror than he probably ought to, and considered his words carefully. "Here's what's going to happen. You're going to go back to your friends and you're going to take them a message."

"Fine, fine," Owen agreed, nodding rapidly. "Whatever you want!"

"Nickel City is safe," Theo said firmly. "You come here, you're declaring war. You may think you know our secrets, but you know *nothing*. You don't understand our power and you don't fathom our resolve. No child, no *shifter*, shall ever be touched here."

"Tell them," Theo said, drawing even closer to Owen's face. "Tell them I know them now. Tell them that shifters are watching, that we are wise to them, and they do not want to be our enemies. If they bring that battle, we will be ready, and they will not survive the first wave of our fury. If they want to hunt us, prepare to *be* hunted. We *will* protect what is ours."

To Theo's surprise, Juliette had ghosted up to Owen's side and stabbed a fist at his neck as he flinched away from her. She was holding a syringe in her hand when she drew it away and Owen swiftly slumped, so that Theo was suddenly holding his entire weight.

"That was an impressive speech, Theo," Juliette said kindly, slipping the syringe into some kind of holster that she had under her coat. Theo realized at that moment that her coat was blooming with blood. "But I'm going to take Owen back to the agency with me. He'll have information that they want and we might be able to use him to get into the corporation."

Theo let go of Owen and he slithered ungracefully to the floor in an uncomfortable-looking heap. There was a feeling in the room of a balloon slowly deflating, everyone's breathing loud and ragged. Addison crouched to put the gun she'd been holding carefully on the floor and sagged to her knees.

Theo looked first to Wendy, who was cradling her stapler to her breastbone in what looked like wonder. "Are you okay?" he asked, before thinking that Addison was probably more rattled, and Juliette had actually been shot. Instinct wasn't suggesting Wendy had been hurt, but she looked dazed and shell-shocked.

Wendy gazed back at him, her eyes wide.

"I think…that there is a lynx in my head," she said in awe.

CHAPTER 38

There wasn't just a lynx in Wendy's head, there was a *noisy* lynx in her head, with a constant stream of observations about everything.

I liked his speech, she said of Theo's bristling warning. *But I would have clawed him up a little first.*

You can't just maul someone, Wendy cautioned.

The Bad Man tried to steal our children! her lynx said furiously. *We should lick them and take his awful scent off them forever.*

I'm not licking Theo's kids, Wendy said.

You can lick Theo, her lynx suggested slyly.

Wendy was amenable to that idea.

"Is your gryphon always this…bubbly?" she asked Theo. "It's like having cotton candy between my ears."

"Your lynx is more bubbly than you?" Theo asked in astonishment.

"What is that supposed to mean?" Wendy demanded.

"You're pretty bubbly," Darius said. "Are you a shifter now?" He was carrying Jackson in his arms, and the baby gryphon was cooing happily.

The hope shining in his eyes matched the hope that was rising in Wendy's soul.

"I am not bubbly," Wendy protested. "And…I don't know."

Of course we are, her lynx said. *Let's shift. I'll show you.*

Hold on to your tufts, Wendy cautioned. *We have to wait until it's safe.*

I know it's safe, her lynx sang. *Instinct says so!*

Instinct, Wendy suspected, might know what was safe, but it didn't know what was *appropriate*. Addison was still looking white as a sheet, kneeling next to the gun she'd carefully put down, and Juliette appeared to be bleeding. As much as Wendy wanted to try the one thing she'd always dreamed of being able to do, there were definitely more important things to be dealt with first.

It was distinctly *odd* having an animal pout in her head.

Theo was still looking at her in astonishment. "Go make sure that Juliette isn't going to bleed out," Wendy told him. "Darius, are you and Jackson hurt? Addison, honey, none of this was your fault."

There was a squeal of truck tires outside the door, and everyone froze, wondering if Owen had called for reinforcements.

Even her lynx was at high alert, not afraid, but quivering in anticipation. The double doors to the DMV flung open together and Roderick raged in, shouting, "Where is he? What did he *do* to you?"

Addison rose to meet him, weeping in relief, and Wendy had to clear her throat and turn away from their passionate reunion as he wrapped protective arms around her. She caught Theo's quick glance, but didn't have enough time to interpret it. He went back to helping Juliette sit down and take her coat off, but continued watching

Wendy from the corner of his eye. Darius, one-handed because of Jackson's wiggly weight, came to help his mother.

Roderick was rocking Addison in his arms, and neither of them had any idea that anyone else was around. Theo's family was concentrating on Juliette, who was trying to assure everyone that it wasn't that bad, that she'd only been grazed, there wasn't that much blood. Darius was appropriately grossed out and enthusiastic about it.

"I'm going to be fine," she promised. "I've been shot up worse than this before."

"Badass!" Darius said in awe.

"Don't swear," Theo reminded him.

Jackson bounced happily and squeaked.

Juliette was their family, Wendy reminded herself, and for a moment, she felt alone in the DMV.

You're not alone, her lynx reminded her. *You've never been alone. I've just been waiting.*

Why? Wendy wailed in her head, the way she never let herself complain out loud. *Why weren't you here with me? I thought…I thought I wasn't good enough.*

If having a cat pouting in her head was weird, having a cat give a very human raspberry was even weirder. *Don't make it all about you! I wasn't ready yet! It wasn't time! Instinct knows when things are right! You did fine without me, and I needed more time.*

Time for what?

The door gave a little jangle and everyone startled, including the very puzzled elderly man holding a pile of forms who looked around the room in alarm. Darius quickly dropped Juliette's coat over Jackson, but it was hard to hide the fact that the sleeve of her shirt was soaked in blood, Roderick and Addison were still locked in a tearful embrace blocking the way in, and Owen was unconscious on the floor.

Wendy was surprised to realize with absolute certainty *that's not a shifter* and she cast around for some kind of explanation to give him.

"Sorry, we're closing early today!" she cried, sweeping past Addison and Roderick to herd the confused man out the door. She realized that she was waving her stapler and seized the unlikely explanation. "We've had a terrible drunken *stapler accident* and we've just got to get this woman to the hospital. Sorry about the inconvenience! We'll be open at the regular time tomorrow morning! Sorry! So sorry! *Really* sorry!" She snapped her mouth closed around another frantic apology and locked the door behind him, swinging the open/closed sign across the window and closing the blinds.

"I don't actually need to go to the hospital," Juliette protested. "I'm going to be fine. Look, it's almost stopped bleeding."

"*Stapler accident,*" Darius chortled.

Jackson was struggling under Juliette's coat and shrieked with gryphon laughter when it was pulled off of him. He shifted into a boy again, and grabbed at the coat in order to play a peek-a-boo game with himself.

Wendy surveyed the damage to the DMV. It wasn't honestly that bad. One of the stands for forms had fallen over, and her desk was a mess, but the plastic chairs that Juliette had done most of her bleeding on were easily wiped off. There were two bullet holes, one behind Wendy's desk that made Theo's mouth go thin and angry, and one in a poster about safe driving that had been behind Juliette. Darius got Jackson dressed from the backup diaper bag that Theo had in his truck.

Wendy took Juliette to the bathroom to help her rinse out her shirt. There was hydrogen peroxide in the first aid kit, and that lifted most of the stains out like magic.

"Neat trick," Wendy said.

"They teach you useful things in spy school," Juliette said wryly. "The coat is a loss, though. The down is soaked."

"I have a hoodie at my desk that you can use," Wendy said.

Wendy held the blouse under the hand dryer as Juliette washed her face and sponged the blood spots off the rest of her clothing. There was a holster she'd been wearing under her coat that had several knives and small pockets. Wendy refrained from asking what it all did. It looked like a Batman belt.

"What will your people do with Owen?" Wendy asked. She had to repeat the question over the sound of the dryer.

Juliette shrugged and winced as it pulled on her injured arm. It was still bleeding, but very sluggishly now and she flipped through the contents of the first aid kit. "We aren't in the business of assassinations," she said firmly, which was a relief to Wendy because she thought she could like Juliette, but she'd be conflicted about that if the other woman was a murderer. "They'll get information out of Owen and see what kind of risk he is, and maybe try to leverage him into working for us under a tight leash. It won't be entirely legal, and I'm not at liberty to tell you any of the details." She softened. "It's safer for all of you if you don't know."

"Let me wrap that up for you," Wendy offered, setting the blouse aside on the counter. The hand dryer went off and left the bathroom in relative silence. "Are you…going to stay here?" she asked reluctantly. "In Nickel City?"

Juliette gave her a thoughtful look and let Wendy take over covering up her arm. It was a little gruesome, and with the blood washed off, Wendy could see that it had gone cleanly in…and not quite as cleanly out. The shot had missed the bone and traveled through a part of her upper arm. An inch to the left would have missed her. An inch to the right would have shattered her bone.

"I'm not going to steal Theo back, if that's what you're worried about."

To Wendy's surprise, she *wasn't*.

He's ours, her lynx purred. *Ours forever.*

Wendy would have called it confidence a day earlier, but now she thought it might be instinct. She knew that she and Theo were meant to be together. Whatever complications they faced, they would figure out how to weather them, because they fit together in some greater way than just mutual attraction and blooming affection. Surly preteens couldn't keep them apart, and sexy super-spy exes wouldn't, either.

"No," Wendy said, examining her own emotions in wonder. "No, I'm not worried. I was just curious how we would all fit together."

Juliette seemed to relax, despite Wendy having to press gauze into the raw flash at the back of her arm. "I'm heading for Alaska for a while," she said. "I'll be laying false trail for them to follow and dealing with some mysteries in that end of the world. I'll miss the kids, don't get me wrong, but Theo's a great dad. I know he can protect them."

"I bet they'll miss you, too," Wendy said, tightening the bandage over the gauze. She helped Juliette get back into her shirt. "And I would have liked getting to know you."

Juliette met her gaze in the mirror and gave a slow

smile. "I'd like that, too," she agreed. "Maybe we can, later."

There was a tentative knock on the door, and then Addison's voice. "Are you guys okay?"

Wendy smiled back at Juliette's reflection. "We're great! Be right out!"

CHAPTER 39

Theo watched Wendy and Juliette go to the ladies' room to get her cleaned up and wondered why he wasn't more worried. His new love and the estranged mother of his children ought to be a recipe for disaster. But he trusted Wendy to make friends with anyone, and Juliette wasn't a bad person, just bad for him.

Knowing what she did for a living certainly clarified a lot of their conflict, but Theo wasn't quite sure he'd forgiven her for keeping it from him. He'd told her what he was—and shown her—when Darius was born. She could have done the same.

But of course, he'd also never told her about teleporting.

Roderick gave Theo a strong shifter-sizzling hand-shake. "If we're not going to turn Owen in to the police, we should probably make it look a little less like there was a shoot-up in here."

They righted the literature stands and stanchions, and roughly organized the brochures. Theo gathered up the files he'd dropped. Juliette's blood—there was more of it than Theo was happy to see—was mopped up with copious paper towels and cleaning solution.

Darius found a "Look Twice, Save a Life" sticker and boldly applied it to the hole in the safe driving poster. "It looks like it was meant to go there!" he said.

The hole behind Wendy's desk was more complicated, but Roderick produced a hammer and nails from his truck and they rearranged the artwork to cover the damage. Theo scowled to think about what might have happened if Wendy hadn't ducked in time. He would not have had the self-control to let Owen walk out alive if he had harmed a single dear hair on her head.

Theo realized abruptly that Owen *had* shot Juliette, and he remembered all over again that the two women were together in the bathroom doing whatever women did in the bathroom.

Trust them, his gryphon advised.

Theo hadn't been this worked up since the day Darius had sprained his wrist and he'd gotten sudden custody of Jackson. His children had been kidnapped, he'd exposed his greatest secrets to a dangerous unknown entity, and the love of his life had been fired at.

Oh, and his ex, the mother of his children, had actually been shot.

Theo had not imagined that a day would come where *that* would be the afterthought.

No one is hurt badly, his gryphon crooned comfortingly. *Juliette will heal. Our chicks are safe. Our mate is whole.*

Our mate. Theo knew the quiet shifter stories about true mates and had always considered them little more than embellished fairy tales for people who needed fiction to explain lust.

Use whatever words you want, his gryphon said impatiently. *She is ours, and she completes us.*

Theo decided he could accept that.

"What are we going to do with the gun?" Darius asked. It was still lying where Addison had carefully set it down. He didn't offer to touch it.

"Take it out to the middle of Belle Lake and drop it in?" Roderick suggested.

"I'll take it," Juliette offered, coming out of the bathroom with Wendy. "My agency might be able to get some information out of the registration." She was carrying her bloodied coat, but her shirt had been cleaned and dried. A bandage showed beneath the bullet hole. She dropped the coat in the trashcan heaped with stained paper towels and Roderick tied up the bag.

Theo looked from Wendy to Juliette very cautiously. "You're okay?"

"And you're a lynx now, too?" Addison added eagerly. She shook out an empty trash can liner as Roderick lifted the full bag out of the way. "Have you shifted?"

"This doesn't seem like the right place," Wendy said, looking around.

"Come to Tiny Paws," Addison begged. "Try it out. We've got a private backyard that's clumsy shifter safe."

"I gotta see this," Darius said eagerly. "Dad, can we go, too?"

Jackson gave a grumpy snort and turned to bury his face deeper into Darius's chest.

"Let's all go," Theo suggested.

"You go," Juliette said. "I need to call in and get Owen to the agency as soon as possible."

There was a finality to her words. This was goodbye.

Juliette zip-tied Owen's hands and ankles and Roderick

and Theo manhandled him out to Juliette's car as discretely as possible. Cold weather at least kept the pedestrians inside, and they weren't on a busy road. Juliette followed them with the files that Theo had brought from the storage unit.

Theo was watching Wendy, not Juliette, so he caught her quick, knowing glance when he returned to the lobby. She hung back so he could say goodbye to Juliette privately, bustling to get her purse from behind her desk and straighten a few things on her desk as Roderick hauled out the trash and Addison followed him.

"Darius…" Juliette said.

"I'm going to miss you, Mom."

Juliette folded Darius and Jackson into a warm embrace. "I'm going to miss you so much. Don't give your dad too much grief, okay? I'll call whenever I can."

Darius said something incomprehensible into her shoulder and didn't squirm away from her forehead kisses. "I love you," she said firmly. "I love you both so much."

"I *mumble mumboo* too," Darius replied.

Juliette smiled sadly at him and ruffled his hair, then cupped Jackson's face in her hand briefly before she turned to Theo.

"I know you'll take good care of them," she said carefully.

They were both keenly aware of Wendy, who was humming as she opened and closed desk drawers very loudly in a clear attempt to keep from obviously eavesdropping. "Lalala, just getting that sweatshirt for Juliette, lalalala. Not awkward at all!"

Juliette cast a sideways glance in her direction and slowly smiled. "She's good for you," she observed quietly.

Theo wasn't going to apologize. "We'll all be fine," he promised. "Go do the good work you're apparently been doing all along."

Juliette winced.

"That's not how I meant it," Theo said quickly, still not making it defensive. "I'm proud of you. Darius is never going to get over the fact that his mom is a spy and he can't tell anyone. I will…always be really fond of you."

"I can't hear anything!" Wendy sang. "Just leaving the hoodie here on my desk and going out to wait in my car because I'm not making anything uncomfortable and I'll lock up when you're done! Don't rush on my account!"

"Wait!"

Wendy froze halfway to the door at Juliette's call, then crab-walked sideways to their party. Darius giggled.

"I'm not capable of not making this weird," Wendy said frankly.

Juliette, to Theo's surprise, actually laughed out loud. "I like you, Wendy, and I like you with Theo. Take care of him for me, okay? Be everything for him that I couldn't be."

"*Everything?*" Wendy asked. "Okay, that's too weird even for me. I'll make sure he wears a hat outside, but he's probably going to be the one keeping me out of trouble. Also, I might drop your baby."

"Jackson will be able to fly pretty soon, so that won't be a problem for long," Juliette said, giggling. "I trust you."

"I trust you, too. If you want a goodbye hug, I'm not going to be jealous."

Theo and Juliette eyed each other and managed a careful hug after one false start.

"Alright, alright, break it up already," Wendy said, laughing, as they were already stepping apart. "I guess I'm a little jealous. Addison is waiting for us at Tiny Paws, and I am dying to see if I can actually shift. Also, do earplugs shut your own animal out, or is this constant commentary just going to be a part of my life now?"

"You get used to it," Theo promised, taking her hand. "I won't promise that it will get any less annoying."

What are you implying? his gryphon wanted to know.

Juliette slung Wendy's oversized hoodie on and walked with them out the DMV doors.

Wendy locked the doors behind them.

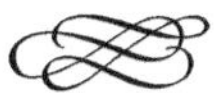

CHAPTER 40

They caravanned over to Tiny Paws and Wendy had to circle the block twice before she snagged a parking space. Nerves fluttered in her chest as Addison let them into the tall-fenced backyard.

Big flakes of fluffy snow slowly fell, and there were only faint muffled sounds of the little city beyond the fence when the gate was closed behind them.

Wendy was aware of everyone watching her. Darius was trying not to look too excited, clinging to Jackson. Theo looked nervous. Addison was bouncing in place. Roderick seemed indulgent. The day care kids were all inside, so at least she didn't have toddlers except for Jackson there to judge her.

Wendy knew how shifting worked. She'd spent so many hours as a kid, visualizing the process, practicing the mental checklist. *Take your clothes. Take what you're holding. Slide into the other shape like water. Think about being…*

It would be more fun without clothes, her lynx suggested.

Stop it, Wendy scolded. *I'm trying to concentrate.*

But the more she thought about it, the more she was

sure she couldn't, she wouldn't. She would fail at this like she failed at everything. She was only imaging this other voice in her head. Her mind had finally snapped because she wanted it so much. Everyone was staring at her, waiting for her to founder.

They aren't waiting for you to fail, her lynx said gently. *They're wishing this for you, too. They want you to succeed. They love you. I love you.*

Wendy felt tears well up in her eyes and in the end, it was as easy as it was swift.

She had to blink several times to understand what she was seeing, and she gazed down at her big, furry paws in wonder and delight. Her clothing wasn't lying shredded around her, so she must have remembered to take it with her. At least Darius wouldn't have the horror of seeing his dad's girlfriend naked to scar him when she shifted back.

Not yet, her lynx begged. *Not yet! I want to play!*

Wendy took a tentative step, trying to figure out how to manage four weight-bearing limbs at once, and found that her body was light and responsive. Too responsive. She almost tipped face-forward into the snow and felt something happen at her shoulders to balance her.

"You have *wings!*" Darius cried. He cleared his throat and said nonchalantly, "That's cool."

Wendy twisted to chase her own body, catching glimpses of huge, feathery wings that seemed to have no weight as she spun. *What am I?*

You are me! her lynx—her gryphon-lynx?—cried happily. *I am you! We are weeeeeeee!*

She pawed at her face to confirm that she did not appear to be half-bird and sent sensation vibrating down her whiskers. Except for the wings, she seemed to have lynx parts everywhere.

Theo shifted and Wendy looked up and up at him. She

was like a kitten next to him; he was the size of a stout horse, and she appeared to be a normal-sized lynx.

She tried to dash between his legs and forgot about the wings and had to figure out how to fold them, falling over in the snow as she tried. It was so much fun being on her back that she wriggled there in joy for a few moments, then sprang up to her feet again. If she didn't think about it too hard, the wings folded down against her back, and she could frolic without them slowing her down.

Can we fly? she suddenly asked.

Yes!! her lynx said. *We should do that now!*

Wendy wasn't used to being the cautious one of a pair. *Someone might see us*, she said reluctantly. *We can't do that right now.*

Her lynx pouted as hard as Darius ever had. Wendy thought about being human again…and then was.

She was abruptly colder as a human and she glanced down swiftly to make sure she still had her clothing on. She did. It simply wasn't as warm as fur.

"That was amazing!" she cried, and Theo shifted back just as she went to throw her arms impulsively around the gryphon's neck. He caught her up in a joyful embrace with human arms, picking her off her feet and spinning her in most of a circle before putting her down with a kiss.

Wendy was divided. She wanted more kiss than he gave her, but she was also very glad they'd gotten past the awkward will-they-won't-they stage and were comfortable with short, casual kisses in front of other people.

More licking, her lynx purred.

No licking, Wendy scolded her.

"You're a lynx!" Addison sang. "With *wings*!" She didn't seem the slightest bit envious. Addison didn't have a jealous bone in her body.

Wendy went around giving everyone hugs, and even

Darius hugged her back. Jackson, in his arms, took a fistful of her hair and babbled in her face.

"Can I have my hair back?" Wendy said, trying to extract it. Maybe it would be easier to cut it until Jackson was older. Ponytails were a thing, too. She could see why Cherry did that.

"Does this mean I still might be a shifter, too?" Darius asked wistfully. "Do I have to wait until I'm ancient, like you?"

"I'm thirty-six, you little snot. That is not *ancient!*"

Neither of them was very serious. Wendy was too happy to be mad, and Darius was too full of hope.

"Maybe it's a butterfly cocoon thing," she added. "Like those inspiration posters are always going on about. It takes a little longer to grow wings, or something."

"You deserve them," Darius said quietly.

Wendy gave him a second hug and had to get her hair out of Jackson's tiny fist all over again.

CHAPTER 41

It was probably against the terms of Veronica Chase's rental agreement to host community meetings, but since Tiny Paws was the safest place in Nickel City for shifters to gather, it was a natural place for the first impromptu shifter safety meeting the following week. The day care was crowded with shifter parents and a few humans.

Wendy was still getting used to her lynx and the prickly pressure of instinct. Juliette, back from Las Vegas for a last visit with her kids before going on to Alaska, was a weird blank space to that sensation, much like Cherry, Vivian, and Chloe. Almost everyone else had a static electric sensation. If she closed her eyes, she could still sense the shifters nearby. Olivia felt like a humming bank of fluorescent lights and Ian, beside her, felt only hot. The cute doctor with Vivian felt tickly.

"If anyone asks, it's a birthday party," Cherry said cheerily. "Does anyone have a birthday we could be celebrating?"

Theo shot Wendy a sideways look, but didn't volunteer her, to her relief.

Wendy grinned at him. "I already got my birthday present," she whispered to him. She didn't clarify whether she meant her lynx, the whimsical box of gourmet chocolate-covered ants (with no legs) Theo had given her, or the hot clandestine sex that they'd had that morning while Jackson slept in and Darius took a long shower.

Theo, natural showman that he was, kissed Wendy and then introduced Juliette to the room.

The others eyed her with natural suspicion.

"I'm not a shifter," Juliette said, answering their unspoken question. "My name is Juliette Catellier and I work with a federal shifter protection agency out of Las Vegas. I've been investigating a group of scientists who have been attempting to unlock and monetize the genetic secrets that you collectively hold. It is not a particularly moral group of scientists, and they've been capturing shifters to study. They are apparently not above kidnapping children."

Most of her audience had already known about the attempted capture of Theo's children, but there was shock and surprise from the others. Many anxious glances were cast towards the back door where the children were playing, and there was a swirl of angry conversation.

When the murmurs died down, Juliette continued. "It's getting harder and harder to keep your secrets as technology gallops along and surveillance becomes cheaper and easier and more ubiquitous. A camera was found outside of Tiny Paws and fortunately disabled, but finding it was only luck, and we can't rely on good fortune.

Juliette sat as Theo told the story of Darius and Jackson's capture and rescue, glossing over the specific mechanics of his teleportation. Wendy watched his face as he spoke, and wasn't surprised when he finally rubbed his face. "I'm not explaining everything," he said honestly, looking around. He didn't apologize. "It's hard to be frank about something you're trained you have to keep hidden, even among others like you. Juliette says there are shifters working for these people, which means that even *shifters* aren't safe."

"We don't have to know *everything*," Olivia said, exchanging a knowing look with Ian. "We just have to know that we all have secrets that need to be protected."

"And kids," Roderick growled, looking at Addison. "I don't like the idea of Nickel City being a target."

Addison took Roderick's hand. "Nickel City is safe. It has the protection of a powerful life elemental, and a considerable array of shifter citizens that will take care of our own."

It was Cherry who spoke up then, looking serene and a little sad where she was sitting cross-legged on the floor. "When I started Tiny Paws, I knew I would provide a valuable service to a community in need. You welcomed me and have trusted me with your most precious treasures. I am not giving up on our shared dream of safety and secrecy. If anyone comes to this day care with ill will, they'll have a helluva fight on their hands. I may not be magical, but I will protect your children with every ounce of my being." It was hard to picture Cherry fighting, but impossible to doubt her words.

She talked them through the additional security she was implementing and they discussed at some length safety protocols and points of contact.

The sound of a door slamming open and a wave of cold air preceded a stampede of little feet, gamely herded by the older kids. "We're cold!" Gil hollered. "I lost a boot!" He was also missing a mitten and his hat.

It marked the end of the informal meeting, and everyone broke into smaller clusters of conversation to compare stories and plot safety measures.

Theo was deep in conversation with Ian and Roderick as Olivia and Addison cornered Wendy.

She knew what they wanted to talk about; Theo had warned her what was coming.

"I'm starting an art co-op in the spring," Olivia said. "Addison tells me you're quite a painter and crafter, and we have a pretty big space to fill."

Wendy raised an eyebrow at Addison. "I don't know. I only do art for fun and to piss off the homeowner's association. I don't know if anything would actually sell."

"They don't have to," Olivia said kindly. "And honestly, wouldn't it piss off the homeowner's association even more if you sold tree sweaters to everyone?"

Olivia knew exactly how to win her over. Wendy grinned. "I'm in! Tree sweaters for everyone!"

"Your paintings and sculptures, too?" Addison prodded. "We'll have a lot of space to fill up."

"I can take up space," Wendy said wryly. "That's honestly what I'm best at." She ducked her head sheepishly. "Yeah, okay. I'll go through what I've got and get some paintings framed up for you."

"This is your fault," Wendy said, bumping her hip against Theo as they left. "I would never have had the courage to do this on my own."

Theo looked at her and furrowed his brow. "I don't want to talk you into doing something you don't want to. If it makes you uncomfortable, you don't have to do it." His truck was parked close to the day care; Wendy's car was several blocks over.

Wendy looked up at the low gray clouds, lingering as Darius got into the passenger seat and Theo went to put

Jackson in the back. "For a long time, it was my dream to be famous for my art. I wanted glory and success and fame, you know? But I never thought I was good enough, and I was scared that trying would mean I'd have to face failure. And I worried that I'd sell out, that it would be a non-stop hustle. In the end, I was a coward. It was just easier to work at the DMV."

"There's nothing wrong with doing things for the love of it," Theo said seriously as he stood up from buckling Jackson in. "There's also nothing wrong with doing it commercially. Just make your art and sing your songs and be your authentic self and be okay with everything that makes you who you are! I love all the parts of you, you weird, wild woman."

"Want to be my business manager?" Wendy said. "You seem to have a knack for selling things."

"What have I sold for you?" Theo asked, shutting the door on a fussing Jackson. Darius was leaning back from the front seat to distract him with a toy.

"Myself," Wendy said. "I never saw myself the way you do!"

Theo took her mittened hands in his and smiled down at her. "Then use me as a mirror, and you will always be beautiful. Ready to go test your wings?"

"Can we gooooooo?" Darius wanted to know. "No smooching!"

CHAPTER 42

"Don't expect it to make perfect sense," Theo reminded Wendy. "It doesn't. Birds have to have hollow bones to fly successfully, and we don't. It's not just air drag and lift and foil physics. There's something else that matters, and you just have to trust that it will work. Let your lynx take the wheel. She'll know how to make it happen."

"Great, more fuel for her superiority complex," Wendy groaned.

"Are you ready?"

Wendy sucked in her breath. "We're ready."

They were standing together at the top of the sledding hill at Belle Lake. It wasn't a day that it was publicly open, but Isadora, the dryad that ruled the forest for miles around, had made it clear that shifters could come and safely romp in this place at will. It was free of prying eyes and in a little hollow that meant there was even air space for private flying.

Addison had told them about the clearing, but she

hadn't explained why she knew it was good for flying lessons.

It was also a perfect place for sledding, with a long slope with varying steepness that ended in a bank of fluffy snow.

Darius, standing at the bottom of the slope, had Jackson in his arms and was bouncing him in place to distract him. The gryphon was trying to chew on Darius's furry zipper pull.

"How do I start?" Wendy asked. She was full of nervous energy, even more than usual.

"Well, first, you'll need wings." Theo shifted to set an example, and stepped away to get space to spread his wings. It felt good to stretch them; he didn't get to be a gryphon nearly as often as he wished he could.

Wendy shifted beside him, into a gorgeous plush Canada lynx with giant paws and folded wings. She spread them cautiously, concentrating too hard on one and then the other. She shook her head, tucked them back in, and then unfolded them both at once smoothly.

She purred in delight, repeated the motion a few times, and then bounced in place, clearly ready for more.

Theo rarely thought about how he flew, so it was challenging to keep his motions slow and easy to follow. He crouched and kicked off with his powerful hind legs, adding power with a downbeat of his wings, and then he was airborne, sweeping down the slope and rising at the end to bank back.

Wendy was already small behind him, Darius standing next to her with Jackson almost impossible to see against his coat. Theo flew back around the clearing and watched Wendy gather herself and spring into the air. She almost forgot to open her wings, and then snapped them out, just before she would have wasted the loft she'd gained from her acrobatic leap. Snow swirled away beneath her, and she soared up into the sky after Theo.

She took to it naturally, instinct and her animal guiding her to understanding how and when to beat her wings, how to use the wind and when to bank. She was smaller and slower than Theo in the air, but no less athletic. It wasn't long before she was doing barrel rolls and tight turns.

Theo indulged in a loud, happy call that filled the entire valley with the announcement of his joy. He was flying with his mate, and everything felt right in the world.

He angled back to where Darius had sat down with Jackson in the snow to watch them.

Theo landed lightly next to Darius and shifted as he sat. Practice meant that he could morph between his forms fairly seamlessly. Darius made a show of brushing the snow off of himself that had been disturbed by Theo's back-draft. Jackson tried to crawl over Darius's lap to greet him.

"She's pretty good at flying already," Darius observed. They could just see Wendy banking and soaring against the gray clouds, right at the level of the treetops.

Did he sound jealous?

"You could still be a shifter," Theo started to say.

"I know, dad," Darius said in disgust. "'But it doesn't *matter* whether I am or not,'" he mimicked.

"I don't sound anything like that," Theo protested. "And it *doesn't* matter. I don't want you to pin all your hopes on the possibility, and I don't want you to think I love you any less if you aren't."

"Geez, Dad. I didn't bring a barf bag because I didn't know we were going to talk about our feelings. I thought we were just going to go sledding."

Theo opened his mouth to insist that talking about feelings wasn't bad and Darius shouldn't be so constipated about it, then realized that the boy's eyes were sparkling with humor. It was so good to see him happy again, even if he was constantly trying to hide it to be cool.

"Fine," Theo said, in mock affront. "Let's see what this boring old man can teach you about hurtling down ice-covered hills."

Theo scooped Jackson into one arm and grabbed a sled with the other. They both got to their feet and raced for the top of the hill. Theo didn't make any effort to stay slow or let Darius win, but he was handicapped by Jackson and Darius had a head start, nimble as a goat up the packed trail. They jostled elbows at the narrow places, and Darius might have won if Theo hadn't been able to wrestle him down and leap over him, holding his plastic sled over-head like a trophy, Jackson crowing happily under his other arm like a floofy football.

"Cheater!" Darius hollered, springing back up to his feet.

"Wendy taught me how!" Theo cried.

"She's a terrible influence!" Darius retorted.

The terrible influence in question crash landed with them at the bottom of the hill, a streak of grey wings and giant feet that puffed into a snowbank and emerged as Wendy in a down coat and crinkling snowpants.

"Landing is hard!" she wailed, struggling back up to her feet. Her whole face was laughing and full of color. "There's snow down my back!"

Theo left Jackson floundering joyously at his feet and helped her shake the extra snow out of her hood. He had to kiss her because she was so beautiful and alive and *his*.

"No smooching!" Darius insisted.

"He doesn't want us kissing in front of him," Wendy said with a sigh.

"No smooching where he can see us, right?" Theo

lifted the sled to shield them and pulled her close with his other arm. Her mouth was home, the feel of her breath and her tongue and her sweet body up against his.

"That's not better!"

"It's much better," Wendy said, smiling up at Theo in the purple shadow of the sled. "I want to do that again! Can you beat me on the sled?"

"Let's find out!" Theo lowered the sled, picked Jackson back up, and challenged Darius, "Can you beat your old man?"

They raced up the hill and down, over and over again, Wendy flying, the rest of them sledding, until they were too tired to stand up after their last crash and had to lie, laughing, in the snow at the bottom.

Jackson was fading fast, and his excitement over the snow and sledding was swiftly turning to complaint and clumsiness.

"He's about to shift," Wendy warned, sitting up. "Woah. It's weird to know that. It's like an itch that you can't quite find."

"Instinct is a strange thing," Theo agreed, still lying on his back. "You'll get used to it."

"I'll take him to the truck and get him back in his snowsuit," Wendy offered, scooping him up as she stood. "It's too cold out here to be naked."

Theo's trust in her was so comfortable and deep that he remained lying in the snow, looking up at the darkening sky. He didn't feel the slightest obligation to sit up and nervously make sure they got safely back to the truck. Was it instinct, assuring him that everything was going to be fine? Or was it that he had a partner now?

A helpmate.

A *soul*mate.

It felt like his family was complete in a way he'd never imagined was possible.

"Dad?"

Theo rolled over on one elbow. It was getting dark and Darius's expression was an enigma. He was still lying flat, holding his wrist against him.

"Did you hurt yourself?" Theo asked in concern.

"No," Darius said quickly. "No. But you asked how I fell off the bleachers."

Alarm flared in Theo's chest. "Did you get pushed?"

Darius sat up. "No! Not like you're thinking! I mean, yeah, we were pushing each other. They're all shifters, and they…don't know that I'm not. I've let them believe I am. We don't talk about it. So yeah, they were shoving a little harder than they would with a human. But…I could've caught myself and I didn't."

Darius had all of Theo's attention now, and he felt his gryphon flutter in dismay. It was impossible to miss that Darius was moody, but was he destructively unhappy? Had Theo missed important signs of depression or sadness?

"Dar—"

"It's nothing bad," Darius said quickly, probably guessing Theo's train of thought. "I just…really hoped that if I was in real danger, I'd finally shift."

Theo let out his breath, and it steamed like a dragon's in the cold air. "That was—"

"Really stupid, I know."

"If you had—"

"I know! It was right in the middle of the Halloween party! Everyone would've seen me! I thought of that halfway down, believe me."

"Darius, you don't have to be a shifter. It's not the be all, end all. You're great the way you are."

"I know," Darius said gravely. "I know that now. I just

wanted to tell you I wouldn't ever do that again. I know you worry about me, but you don't have to."

Theo felt like his chest was full to bursting. He was so proud. Darius was growing into a wonderful young man, full of emotional maturity and promise. Everything in Theo's life seemed to be taking a shape like one of Wendy's paintings, with beauty emerging from chaos.

"So. Can I have my own phone?"

All the pride came busting out of Theo's mouth in laughter. "Is that what this confession is all about?"

"I'm responsible enough! All my friends have them! I really need one! I'll only play educational games! What if there was an emergency? Mom could talk with me directly."

Theo got to his feet and offered Darius a hand up. "I'll think about it," he hedged.

Darius took his hand and scrambled up, and he didn't resist when Theo pulled him into an affectionate embrace. "There's one other thing…"

Theo was sure he looked skeptical. "What?"

"Stop smooching Wendy in front of me!"

Theo's first Christmas in Nickel city had been absolutely bare bones. They had just moved from Las Vegas and everything was still in boxes. Darius scoffed about getting a tree or decorating. He claimed he was too old for kid stuff, but Theo wondered if he was just trying not to make a big deal out of the fact that they didn't have much money. Making a fancy meal for just the two of them seemed senseless, so all they'd really done was exchange small gifts (much smaller than his gryphon wanted to splurge for) and watch Christmas movies. They popped a bottle of sparkling cider near midnight for New Year's Eve, and Easter had gone completely unremarked.

Theo had a feeling that holidays with Wendy were not ever going to be swept under a rug.

There was a real tree in the corner, behind a baby gate, and when Theo had protested that he didn't have any ornaments for it, Wendy had insisted on bringing over a box. In fact, she brought over three boxes, and hung the tree in glittering festivity. Most of the ornaments were hand-painted, or carved, or cleverly wrought of metal, and Theo suspected she'd made most of them. She also hung a wreath on the door and strung lights, both outside and in.

She hadn't stopped there.

The bathroom decor was all green and red with grinning Santas, and the kitchen had a holly leaf rug by the sink and a whole new collection of mugs.

"You have special mugs for the holidays?" Darius said skeptically when she brought them over.

"Why even have holidays if you don't go overboard with them?" Wendy teased. "I exist to embarrass you."

She smacked Theo on the ass and gave him a noisy kiss on the cheek. Darius fled to his room, making noises of dismay.

To Theo's astonishment, the Christmas cheer hadn't emptied Wendy's house of decoration. She had her own tree, hung with just as many ornaments and also silvery tinsel that she had opted not to use on Theo's tree; Jackson was in a put-anything-in-his-mouth stage and the gate only slowed him down—it didn't stop him. Her couch had Christmas throws and there were so many twinkle lights that even when the overhead fixtures were off, there was enough light to read by.

Her yard was brighter than a landing strip for airplanes, with a massive inflatable Santa and a waving snowman. There were strings and strings of flashing colored lights, including icicles and even plastic flamingos in Santa hats.

"I buy them on clearance every January," Wendy explained as she bustled around Theo's kitchen, putting out her holiday crockery. "The homeowner's association tried to shut me down by limiting how many watts I could use and I switched entirely to LEDs and added even more, just to show them up."

"I would not want you for an enemy," Theo said in awe.

"Aw," Wendy pouted. "But you're supposed to keep your enemies closer than your friends, and I *like* being close to you."

Darius was already in his room with his music on, so there was no one to pretend to throw up except Jackson, who was busy trying to figure out how his feet connected to his legs and what they tasted like.

Theo gathered Wendy into his arms and squeezed hard. "What's even closer than enemies?" he asked.

Wendy wheezed dramatically. "Lovers?" she guessed suggestively. "Siamese twins? Oh, do you think Darius would be properly mortified if we did an awful couple's costume next Halloween?"

Mrs. Royal.

Theo had been planning to wait until after Christmas.

"I talked to Darius," he said soberly.

"About going as Siamese twins for Halloween?" Wendy looked up at him with wide eyes and Theo had to wonder how he'd ever lived without all the laughter she brought into his life. Between Jackson and Wendy, his house was always ringing with amusement, and even Darius smiled more easily now.

Theo was better for having her in his life, in a million little ways. He was more patient and less worried, and he didn't feel like he had to constantly apologize. He didn't have anything to prove to her and she didn't have anything to prove to him.

Whatever he did next in his life, whether it was waiting tables or learning to drive big equipment or playing guitar, he wouldn't have to do it alone.

"Okay, I'm sorry, we don't have to be Siamese twins. We can be left and right Twix or something instead. Or bacon and eggs. I saw a costume for sexy fried eggs once. I swear, costume makers want everything to be sexy."

"Wendy…"

"You can be the sexy eggs, if you want. I'll be the bacon. I'm not committed to gender norms."

"Wendy…"

"This one at least makes a little bit of sense, though, since I've got the eggs and you definitely have the meat."

"Wendy!" Theo had to laugh, and Jackson wanted to be involved in whatever was funny. He gave up on eating his feet and crawled over to pull himself up on Theo's legs and bounce in place. "I'm trying to ask you to marry me!"

Wendy went still, her mouth parted in surprise. She made several attempts at speech and then gave a happy sigh. "Really? *Me?*"

"I already talked to Darius about it and he sort of shrugged and said it would be okay, which is as good as we're going to get from him."

"What about the rug rat?" Wendy said merrily. Jackson was fussing to be picked up.

"He teleports to you. I think that's as sure a sign of approval as you're going to get out of a non-verbal baby."

Jackson gave a squawk and then shifted into his gryphon form, clearly hoping his wings would suddenly prove strong enough to get him up into someone's arms. Wendy stooped and picked him up after some fluttering in vain, tossing him a few inches into the air as she stood.

"Well?"

"A deep shaft full of water," Wendy teased.

Theo didn't think she was dodging his question on purpose, but he was desperate for an answer. "Wendy, will you marry me?"

"Can we get married as sexy eggs and bacon?"

"You can wear anything or nothing and throw rice

cakes and release flamingos instead of doves, if that's what you want," Theo promised her.

"I'll have to think about that," Wendy said. "Flamingos would probably have trouble surviving in the wilds of Montana. Maybe we could do ducks or Canada geese."

"As long as you are at my wedding, I do not care what fowl there is."

"Do you count as fowl?" Wendy wanted to know. "Half-fowl?"

"Stop fowling around!" Theo commanded. "Are you going to marry me?"

"No harm, no fowl," Wendy said, throwing her head back with laughter. "Yes! Yes, I'll marry you! I'll fowl-low you anywhere, you sexy beast."

Theo squashed Jackson between them because he had to kiss her immediately and the baby gryphon gave a shriek of protest and vanished.

Theo and Wendy fell apart from each other in alarm, only to hear Darius shout, "I don't know what you two are doing, but I've got the baby!"

"What are we doing?" Wendy asked quietly as their laughter faded.

"Getting married. Mixing up two of the craziest house-holds in Verona...or at least in Nickel City. Letting the world know that you're mine and I love you."

Wendy's eyes were suspiciously bright. "I...I love you," she said softly. Flustered Wendy was still adorable. "I'd like you to be mine."

It was easier to kiss her without Jackson squirming between them, and Theo did so, thoroughly, until Darius came to the door with a clucking Jackson and made a loud noise of disgust. "Yuck! Stop! I didn't want to see that! Groooooosssssss!"

And everything was just right in the world.

A NOTE FROM ELVA

I loved writing this book so much! I wasn't sure if I could top a fire-breathing, squirrel-shifting toddler (and I'm not sure I did…Lucy is her own force of nature!), but I had a lot of fun throwing obstacles at poor Theo. I also relished bringing Wendy back. She reminds me a lot of me: just as off-the-beaten-path and a lot more outgoing.

This wasn't an easy book to get right, and I am especially grateful to my editors and early readers for helping me polish it into this form. I'm delighted with the end result, even with the extra work, and I'm looking forward to writing a spinoff with Juliette's secret agency in the future. There are a lot of mysteries left to uncover, and this world continues to enchant me.

Questions? Suggestions? Did you find typos? Email me anytime at elvaherself@elvabirch.com!

Continue the story in *Stallion's Instinct*! She's in for the ride of her life!

~Elva

facebook.com/elvabirch

amazon.com/author/elvabirch

goodreads.com/elvabirch

MORE BY ELVA BIRCH

~

A Day Care for Shifters: A feel-good series about adorable shifter kids and their struggling single parents in a town full of mystery and surprise. Start the series with Wolf's Instinct, when Addison comes to Nickel City to take a job at a very special day care and finds a family to belong to. A gentle ice-cream-straight-from-the-container escape. Sweet and sizzling!

~

The Royal Dragons of Alaska: A fascinating alternate world where Alaska is ruled by secret dragon shifters. Adventure, romance, and humor! Reluctant royalty, relentless enemies…dogs, camping, and magic! Start with The Dragon Prince of Alaska.

Suddenly Shifters: A hilarious series of novellas, serials, and shorts set in the small town of Anders Canyon, where something (in the water?) is making ordinary citizens turn into shifters. Start with Something in the Water!

Lawn Ornament Shifters: The series that was only supposed to be a joke, this is a collection of short, ridiculous romances featuring unusual shifters, myths, and magic. Cross-your-legs funny and full of heart! Start with The Flamingo's Fated Mate!

Birch Hearts: An enchanting collection of short stories and novellas. Unconstrained by theme or setting, each short read has romance, magic, and heart, with a satisfying conclusion. And always, the impossible and irresistible. Start with a sampler plate in Prompted 2 for fourteen pieces of sweet-to-sizzling flash fiction, or dive in with the novella, Better Half - which you can get free for joining my mailing list at elvabirch.com!

Shifting Sands Resort: A complete ten-book series - plus two collections of shorts. This is a thrilling shifter romance set at a tropical island resort. Each book stands alone but connects into a great mystery with a thrilling conclusion. Start with Tropical Tiger Spy or dive in to the Omnibus edition, with all of the novels, short stories, and novellas in my preferred reading order! This series crosses over with *Fire and Rescue Shifters* and *Shifter Kingdom!*

Fae Shifter Knights: A complete four-book fantasy portal romp, with cute pets and swoon-worthy knights stuck in a world of wonders like refrigerators and ham sandwiches. Start with Dragon of Glass!

Green Valley Shifters: A sweet, small town series with single dads, secret shifters, sweet kids, and spinsters. Low-peril and steamy! Standalone books where you can revisit your favorite characters - this series is also complete with six books! Start with Dancing Bearfoot! This series crosses over with **Virtue Shifters**, which starts with Timber Wolf.

BEHIND THE SCENES

What is Patreon?

Patreon is a site where readers and fans can support creators with monthly subscriptions.

At my Patreon, I have tiers with early rough drafts of my books, flash fiction, coloring pages, signed and sketched paperbacks, exclusive swag, original artwork, photographs…and so much more! Every month is a little different, and there is a price for every budget. Patreon allows me to do projects that aren't very commercial and makes my income stream a little less unpredictable. It also gives me a place to connect with my fans!

Come find out what's going on behind the scenes and keep me creating at Patreon! patreon.com/ellenmillion